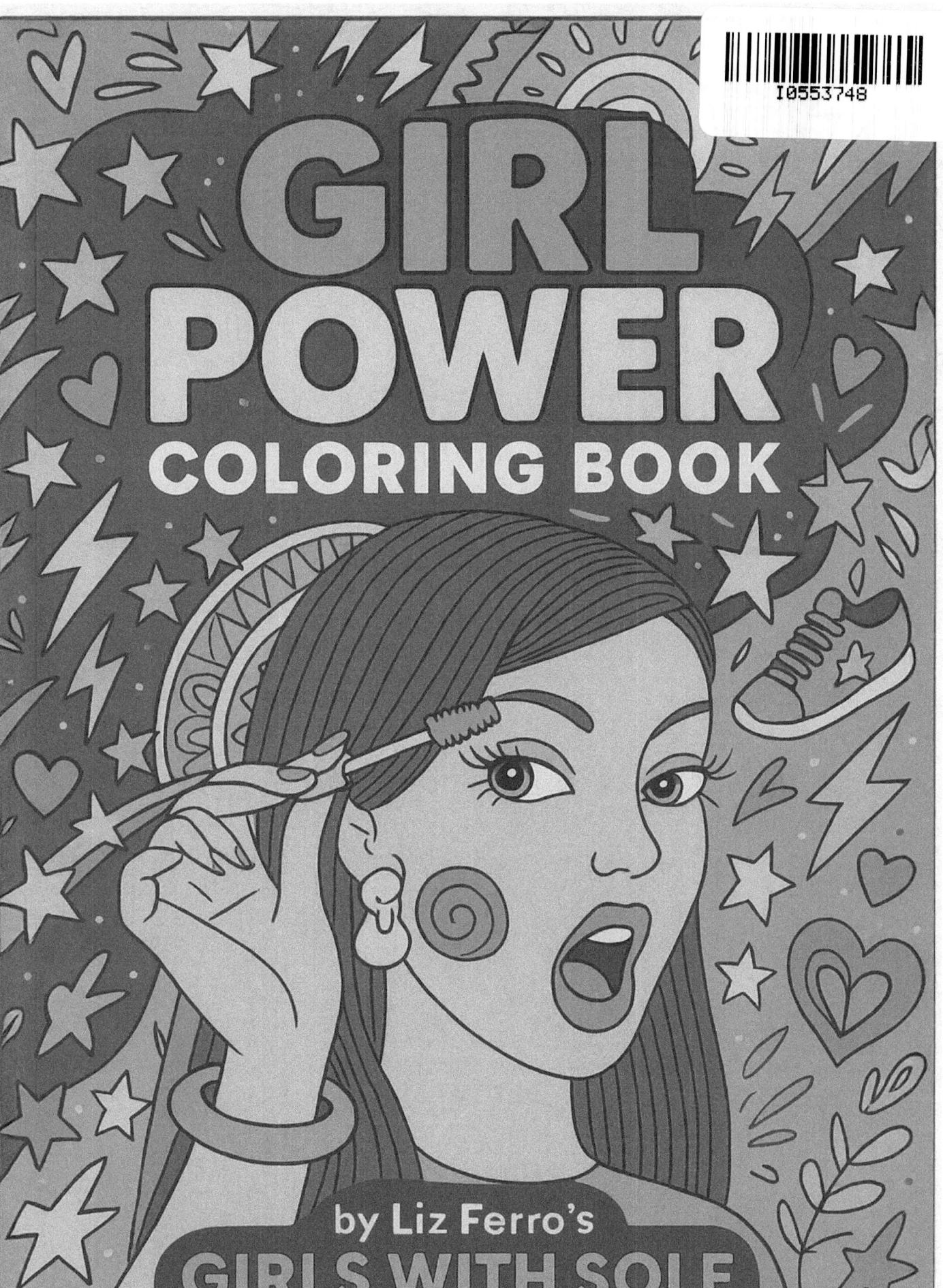

GIRL POWER
COLORING BOOK

by Liz Ferro's
GIRLS WITH SOLE

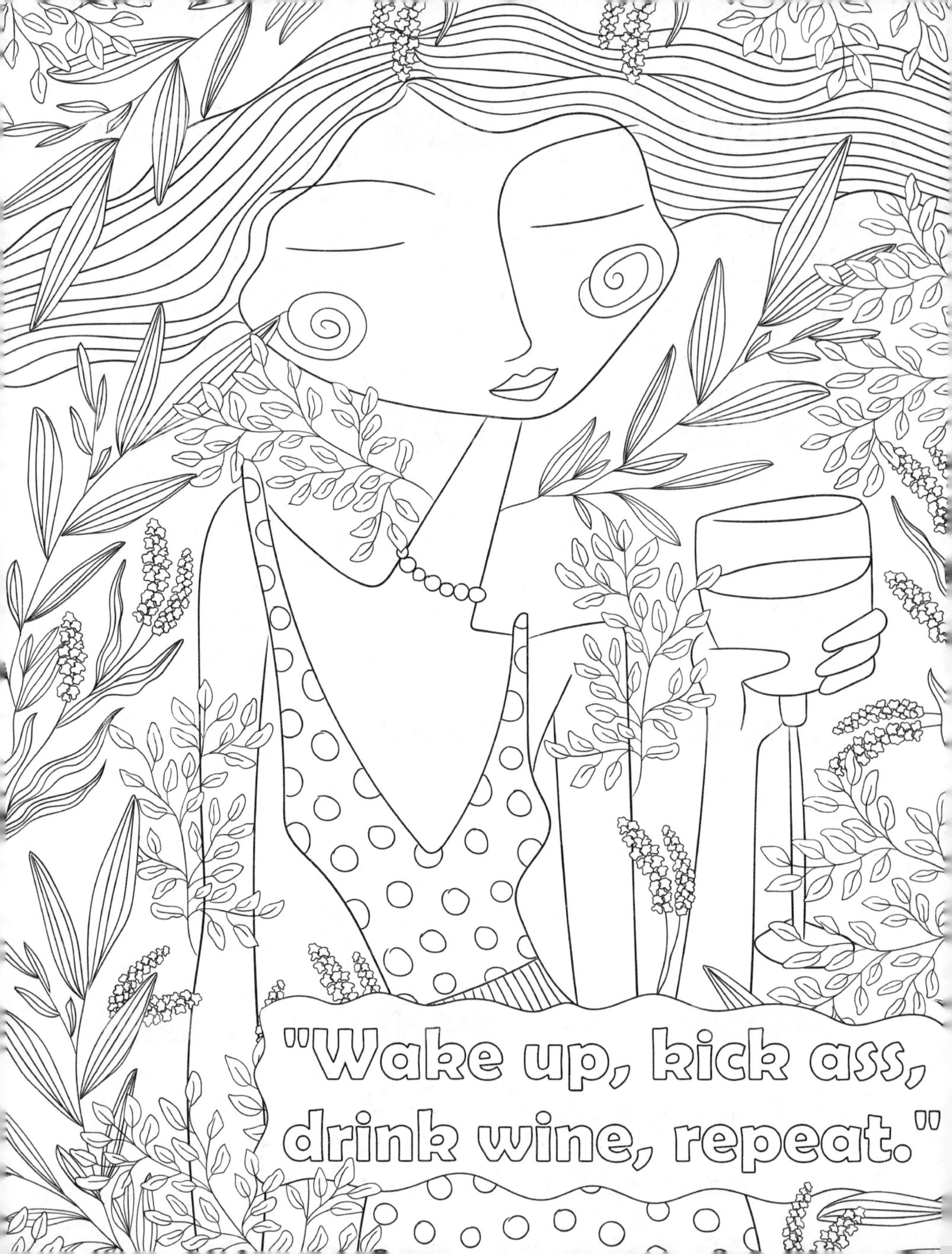

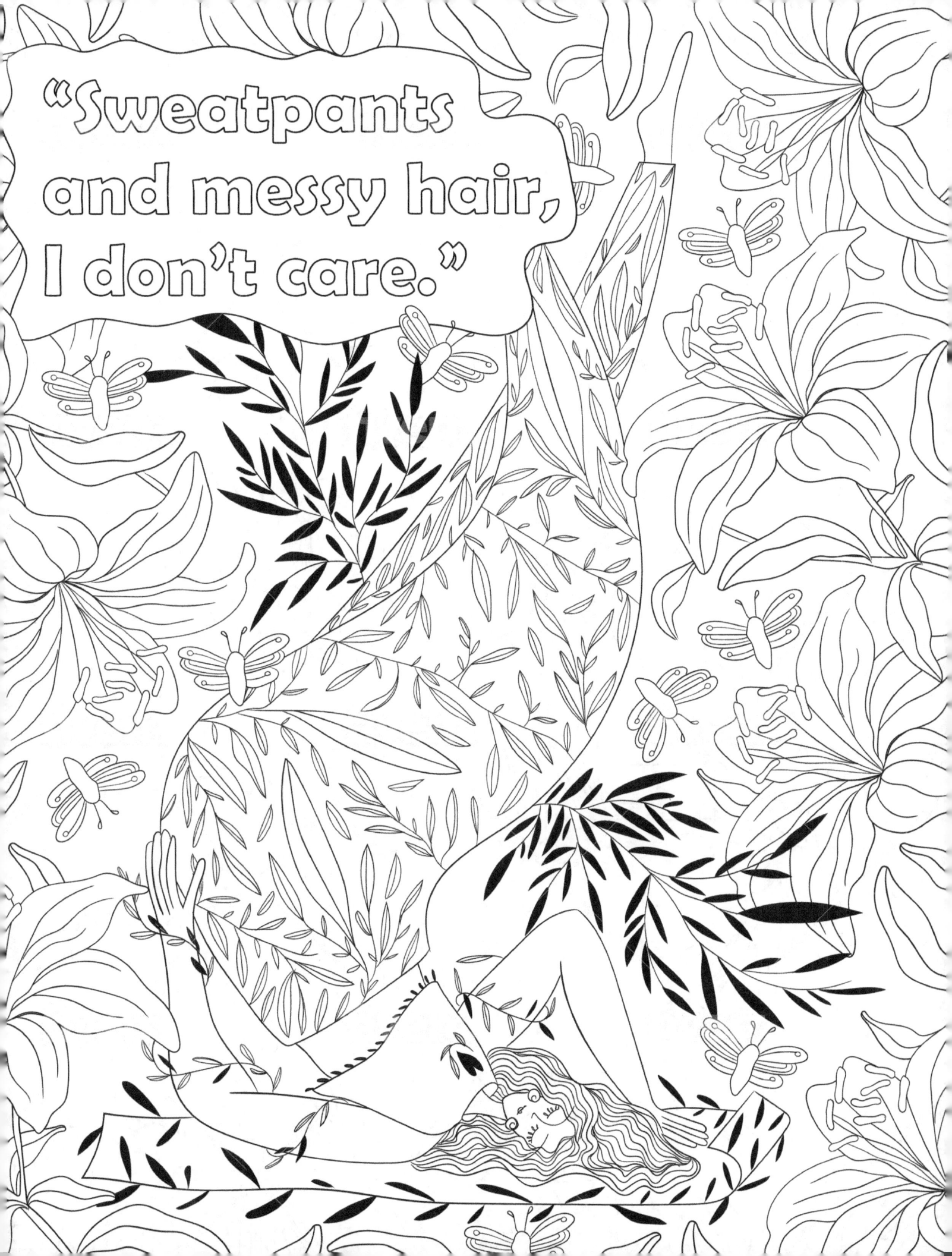

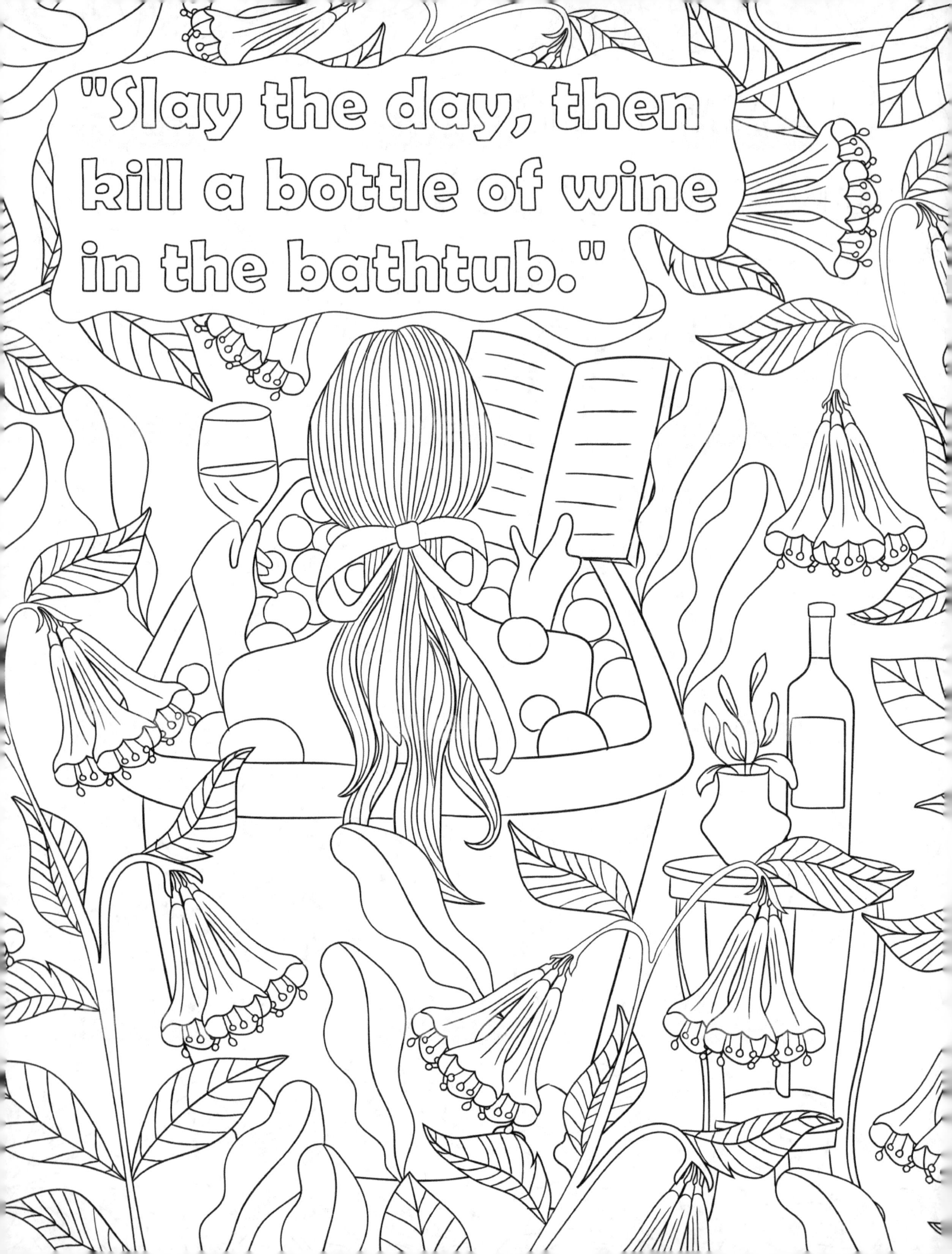

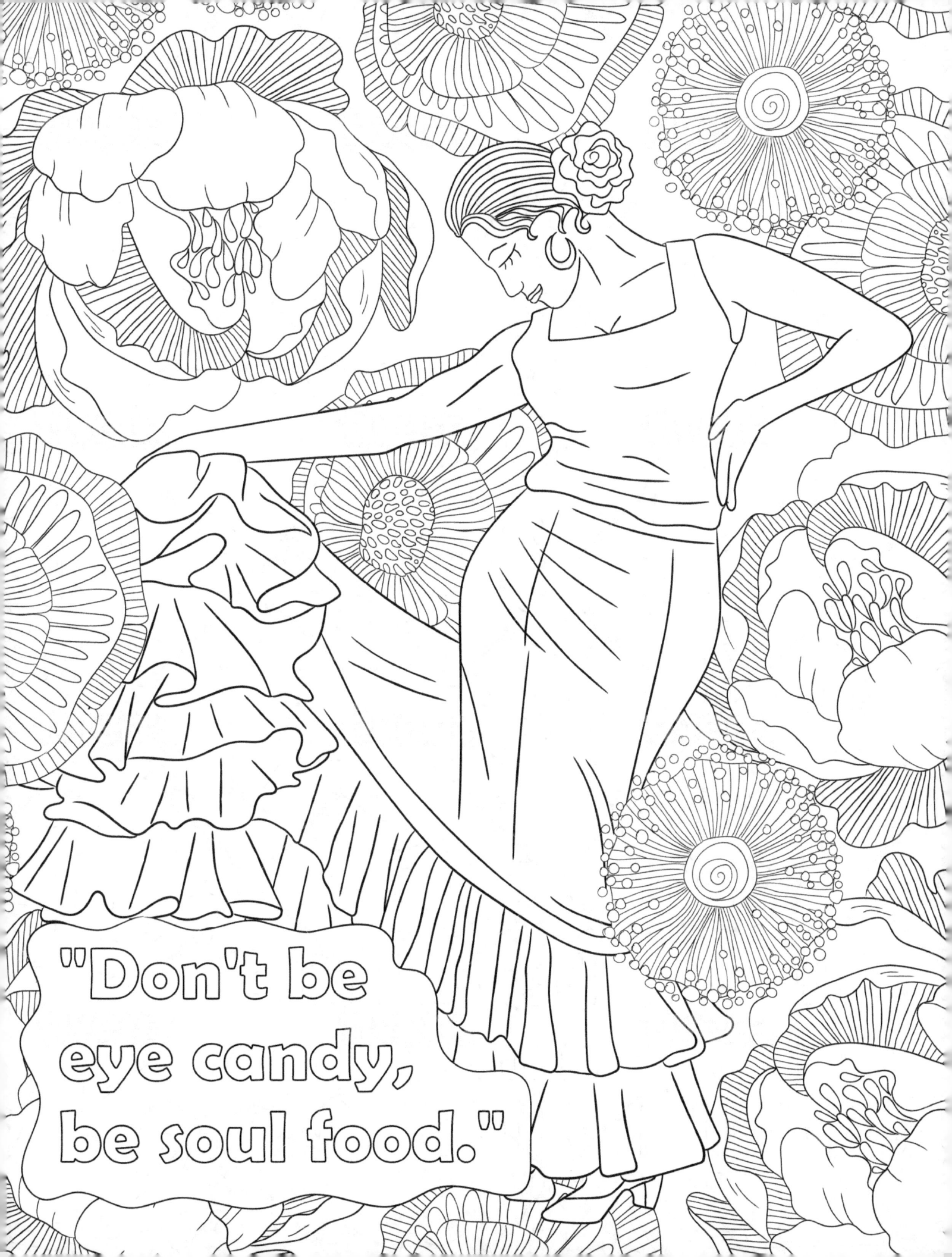

"Don't be eye candy, be soul food."

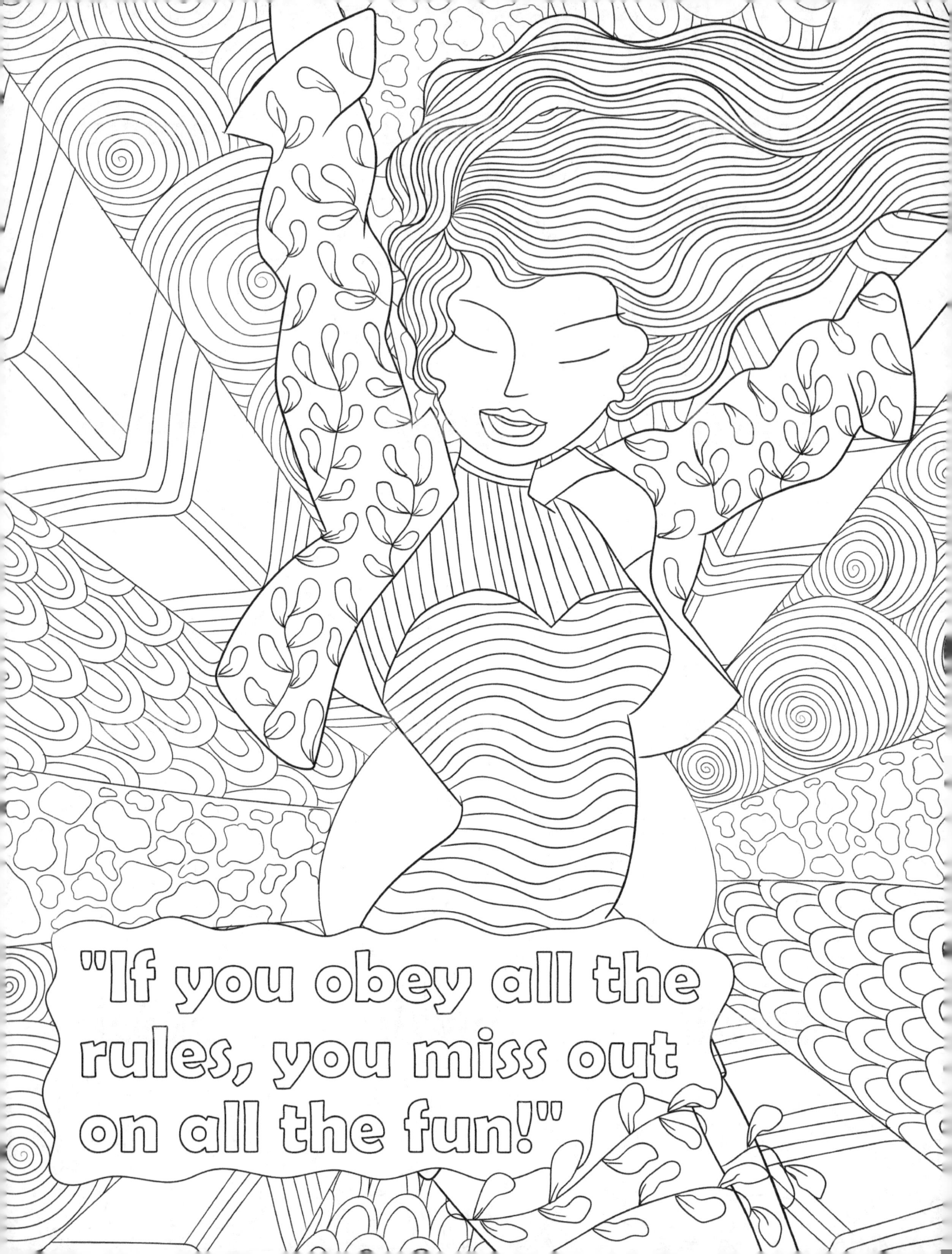

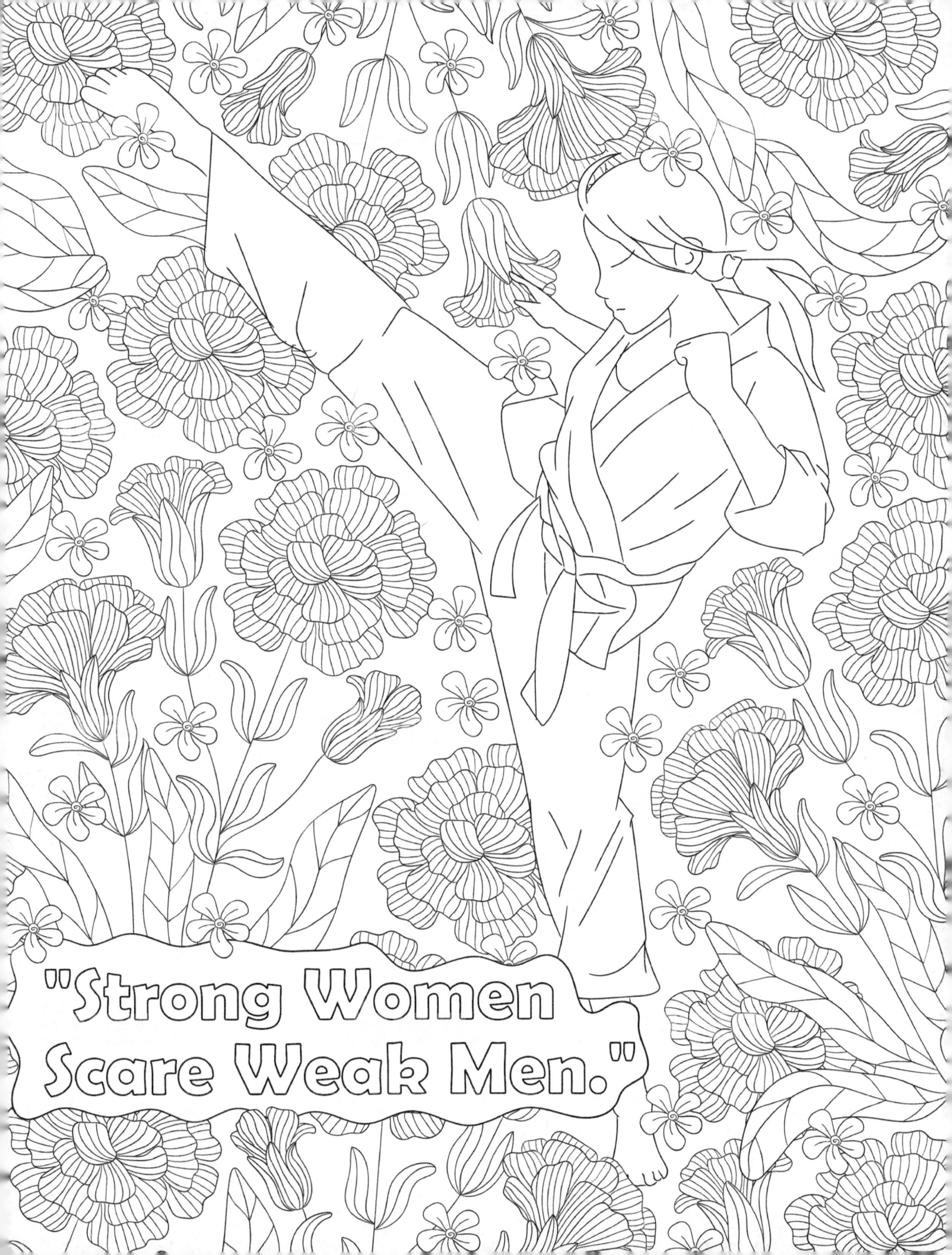

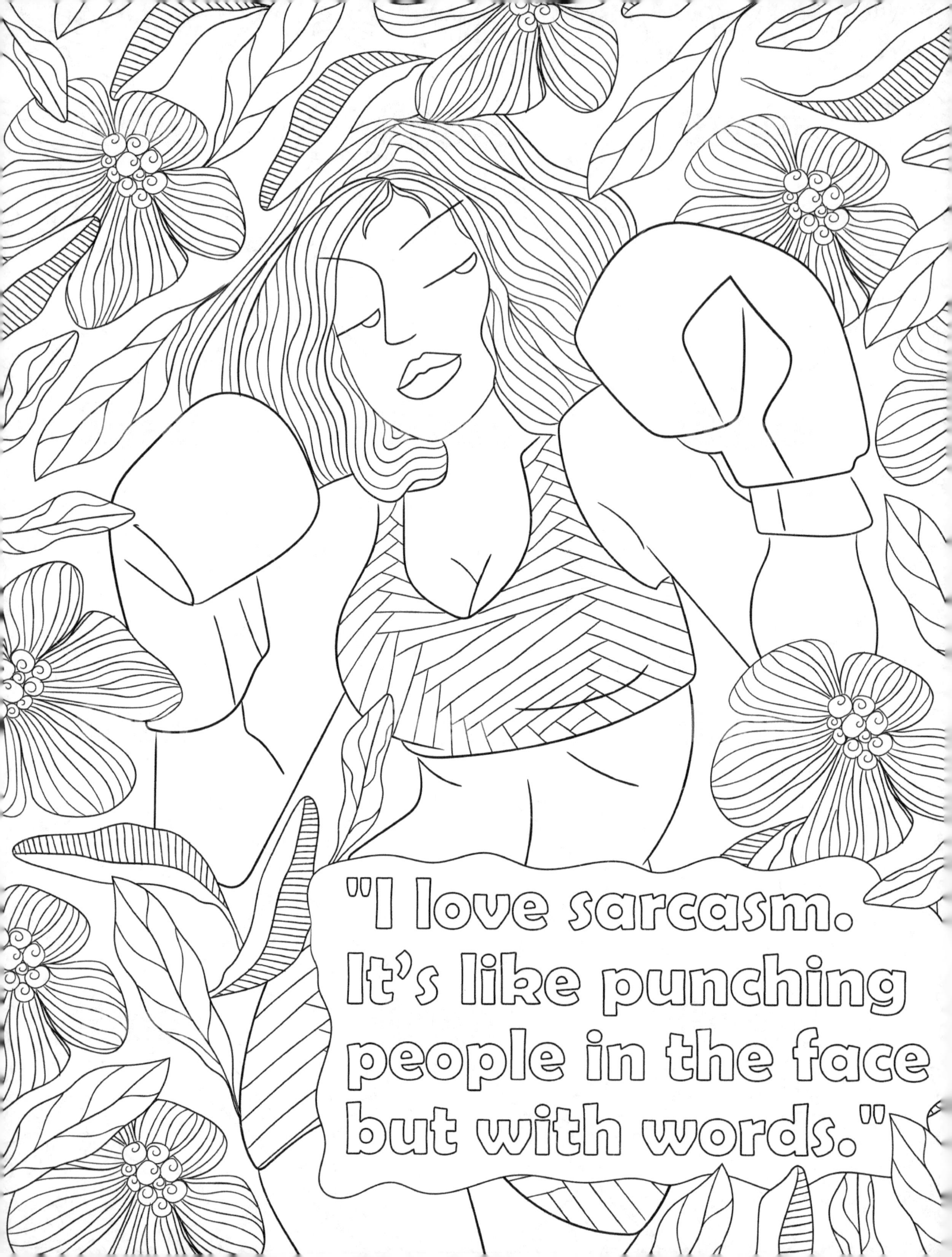

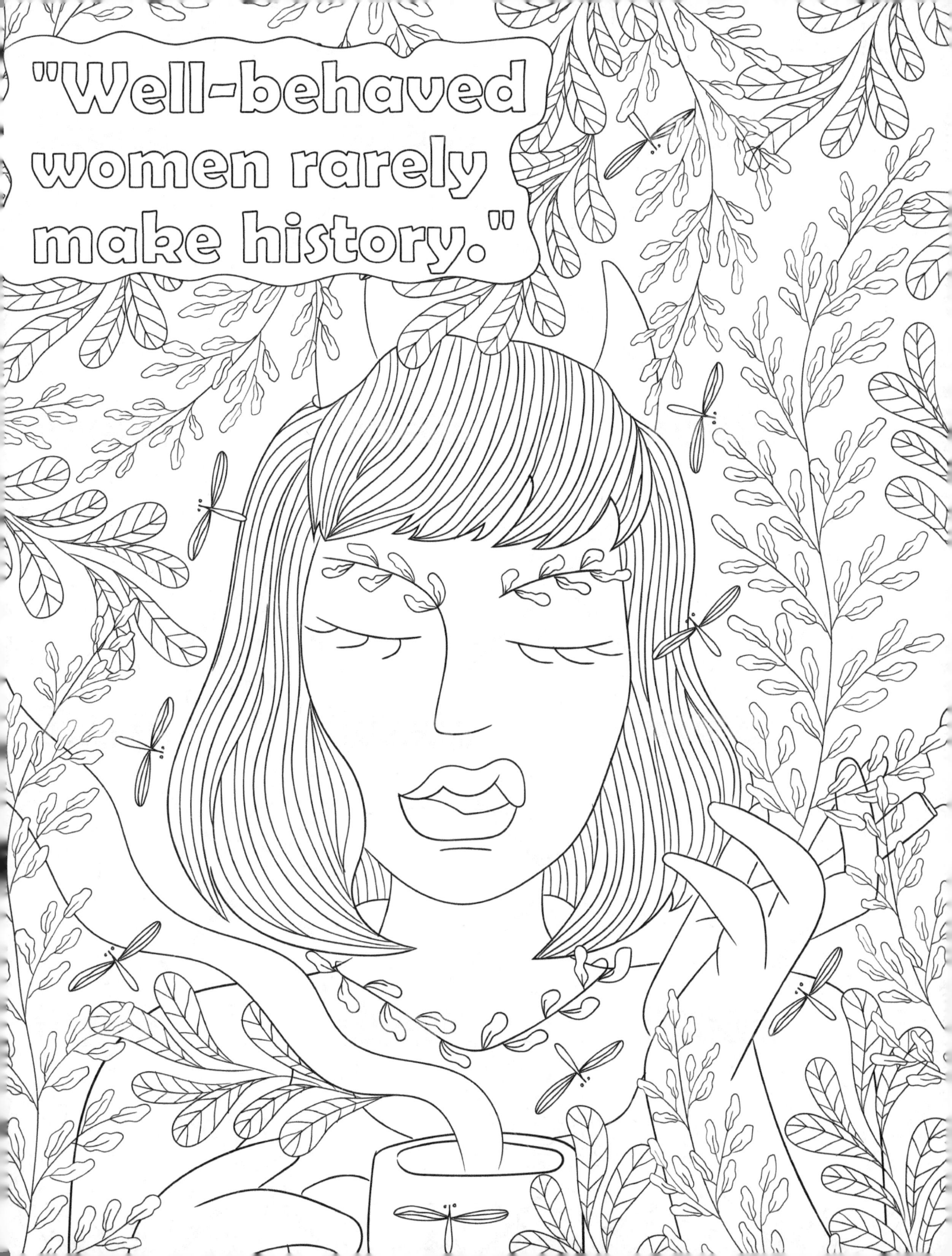

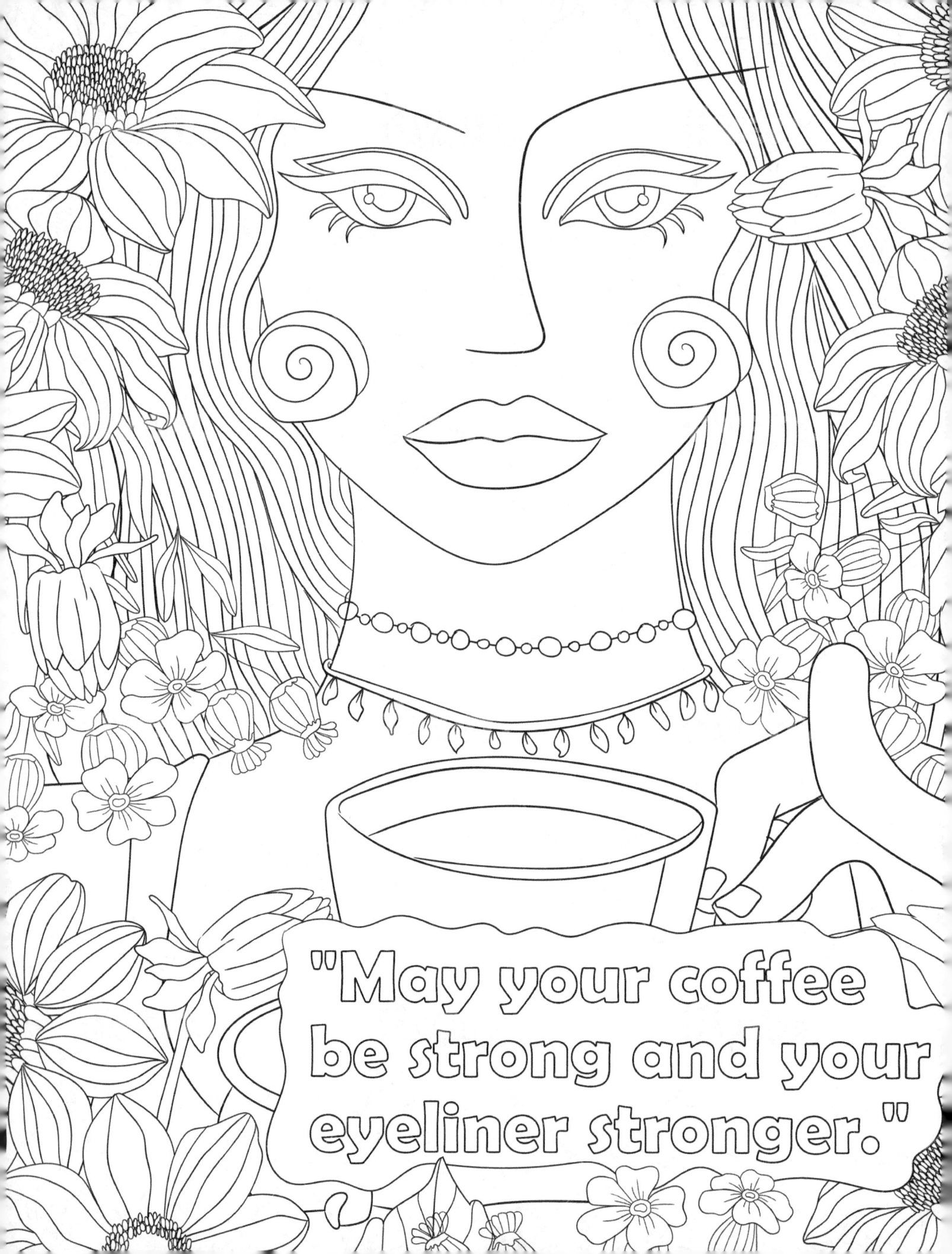

"May your coffee be strong and your eyeliner stronger."

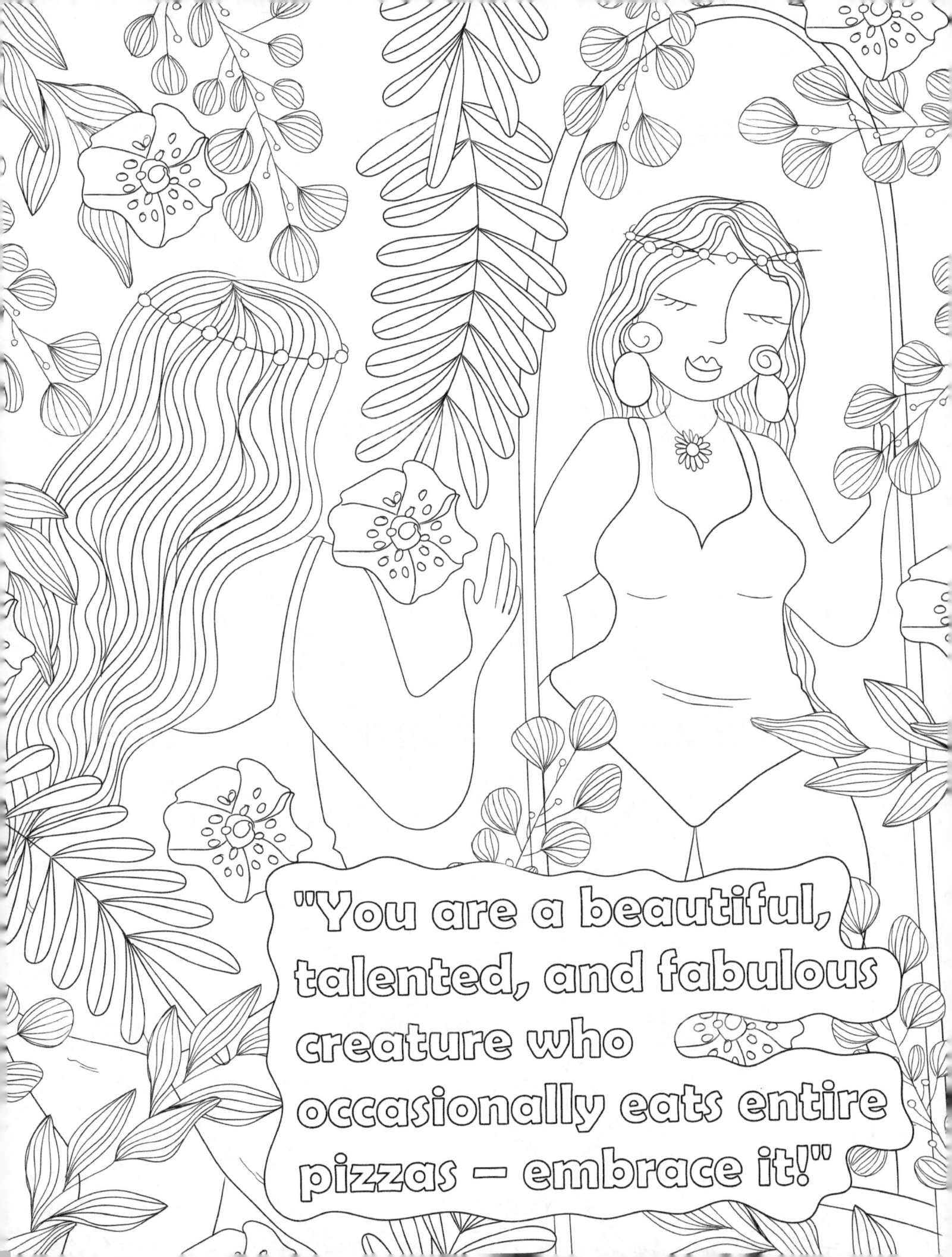

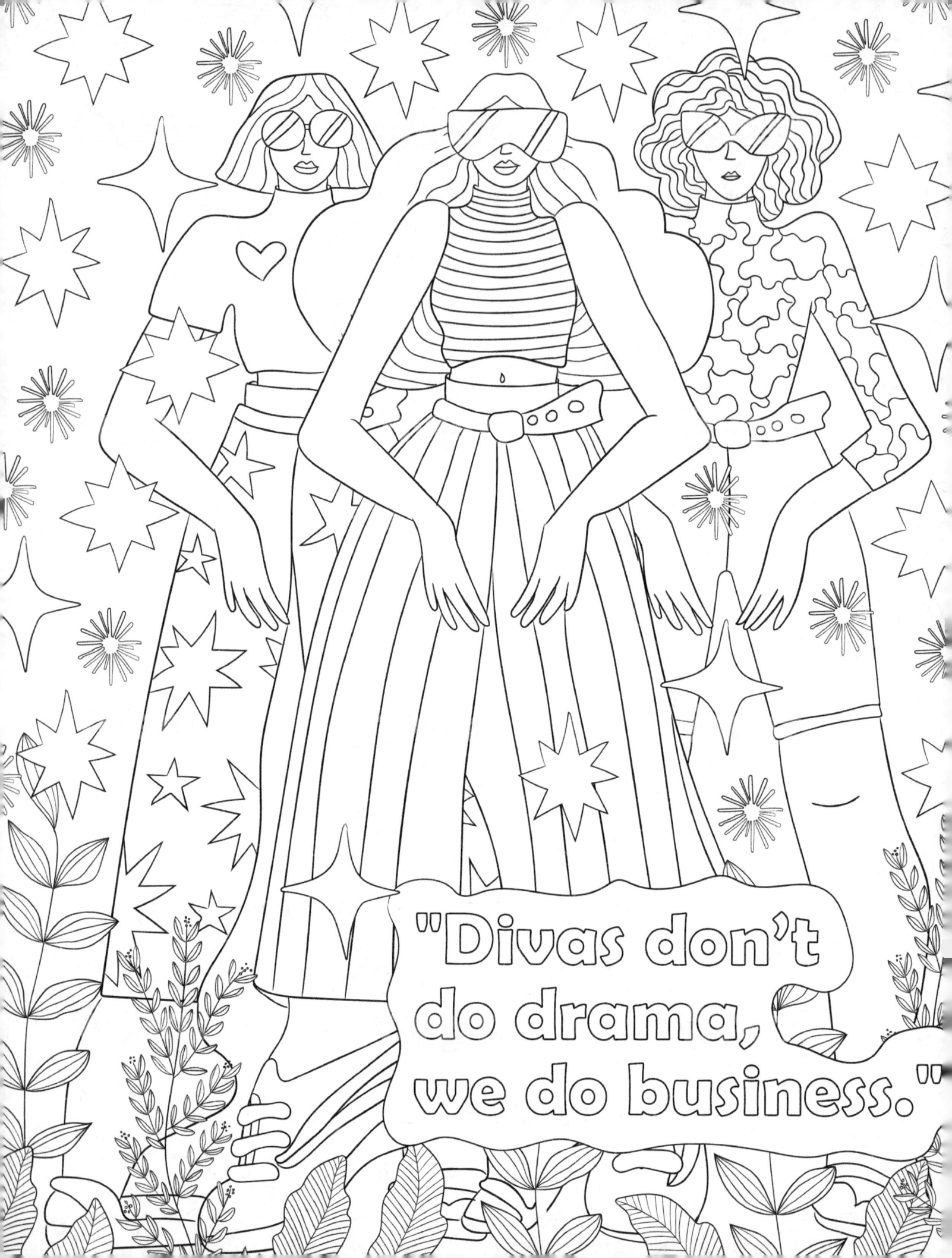

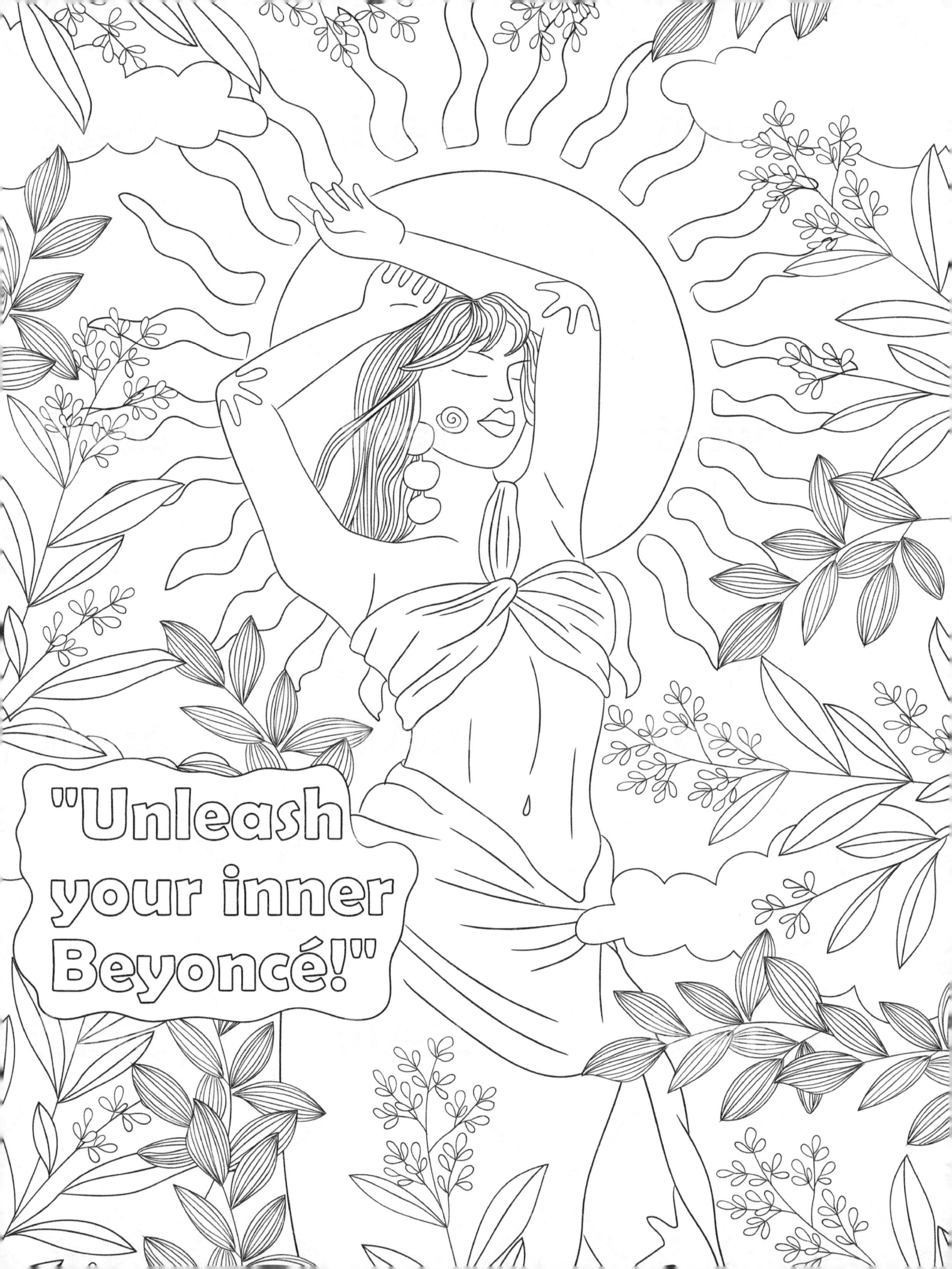

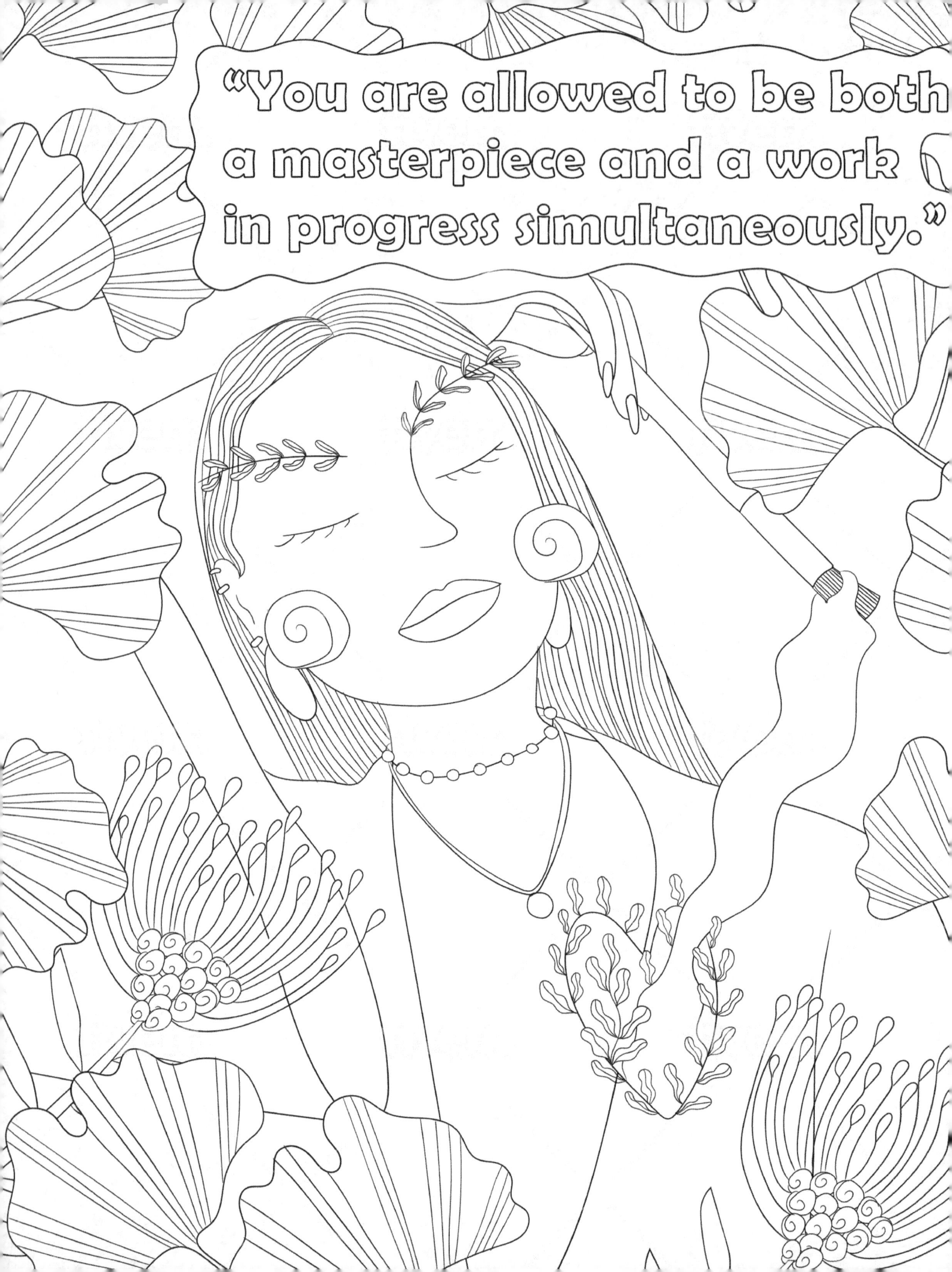

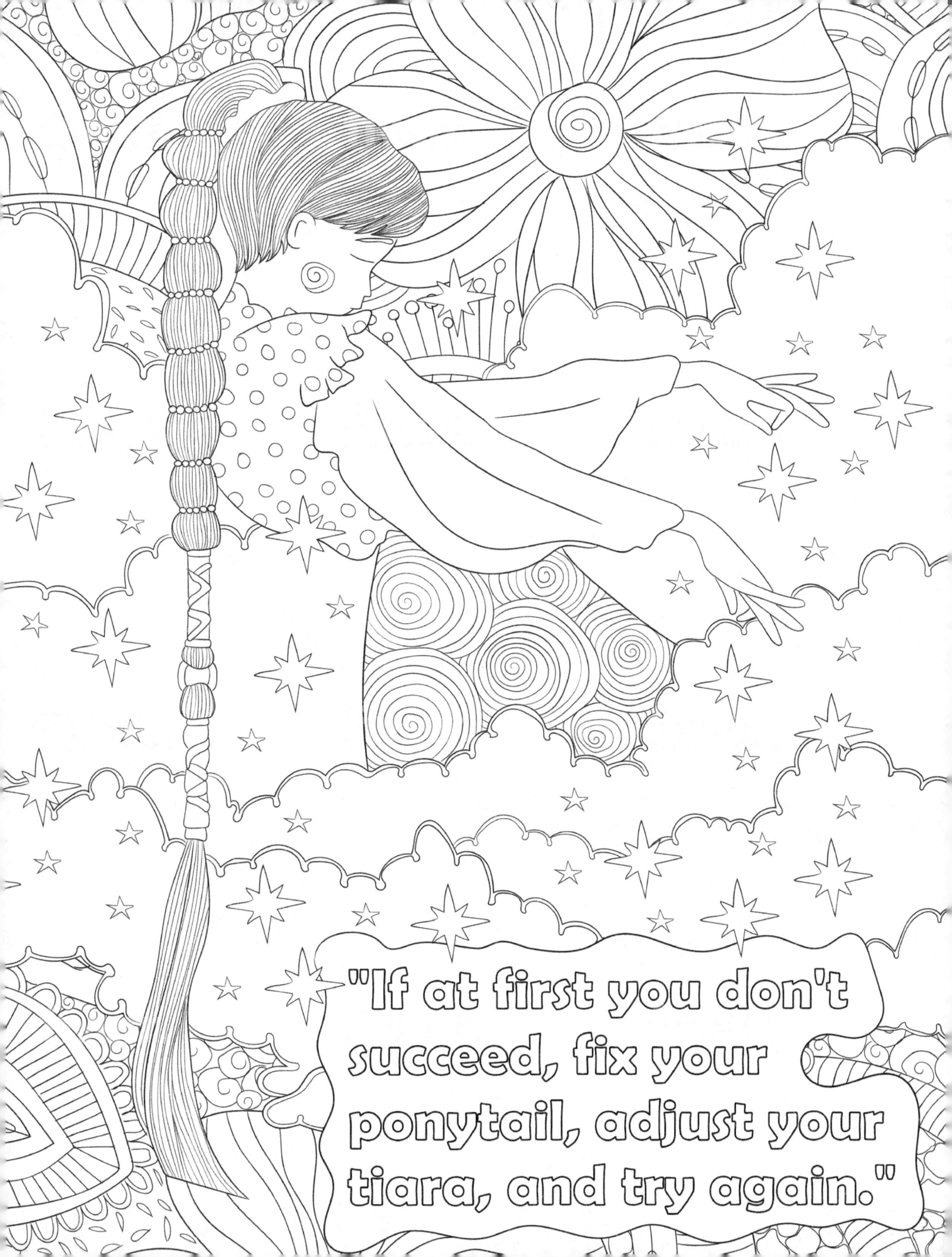

"If at first you don't succeed, fix your ponytail, adjust your tiara, and try again."

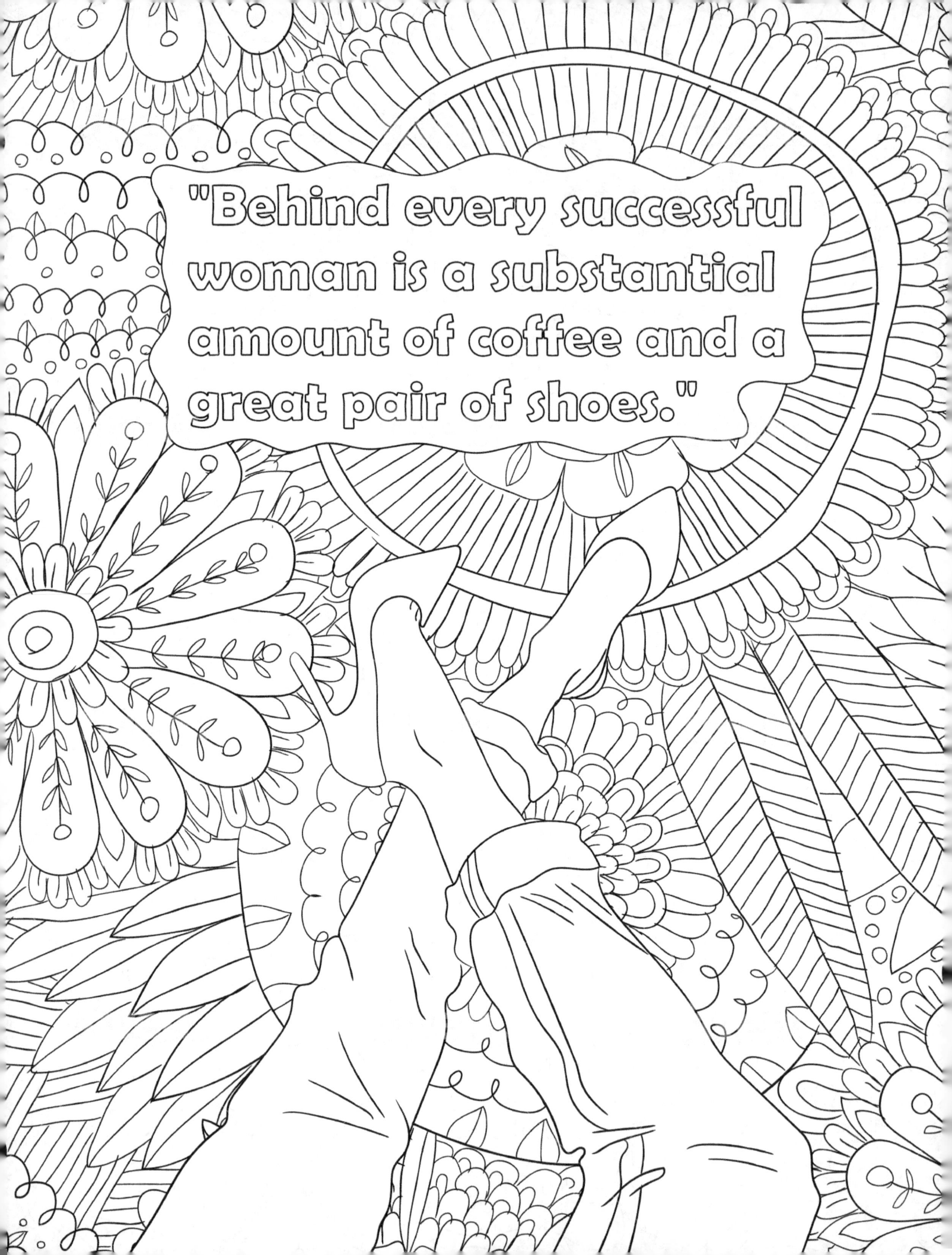

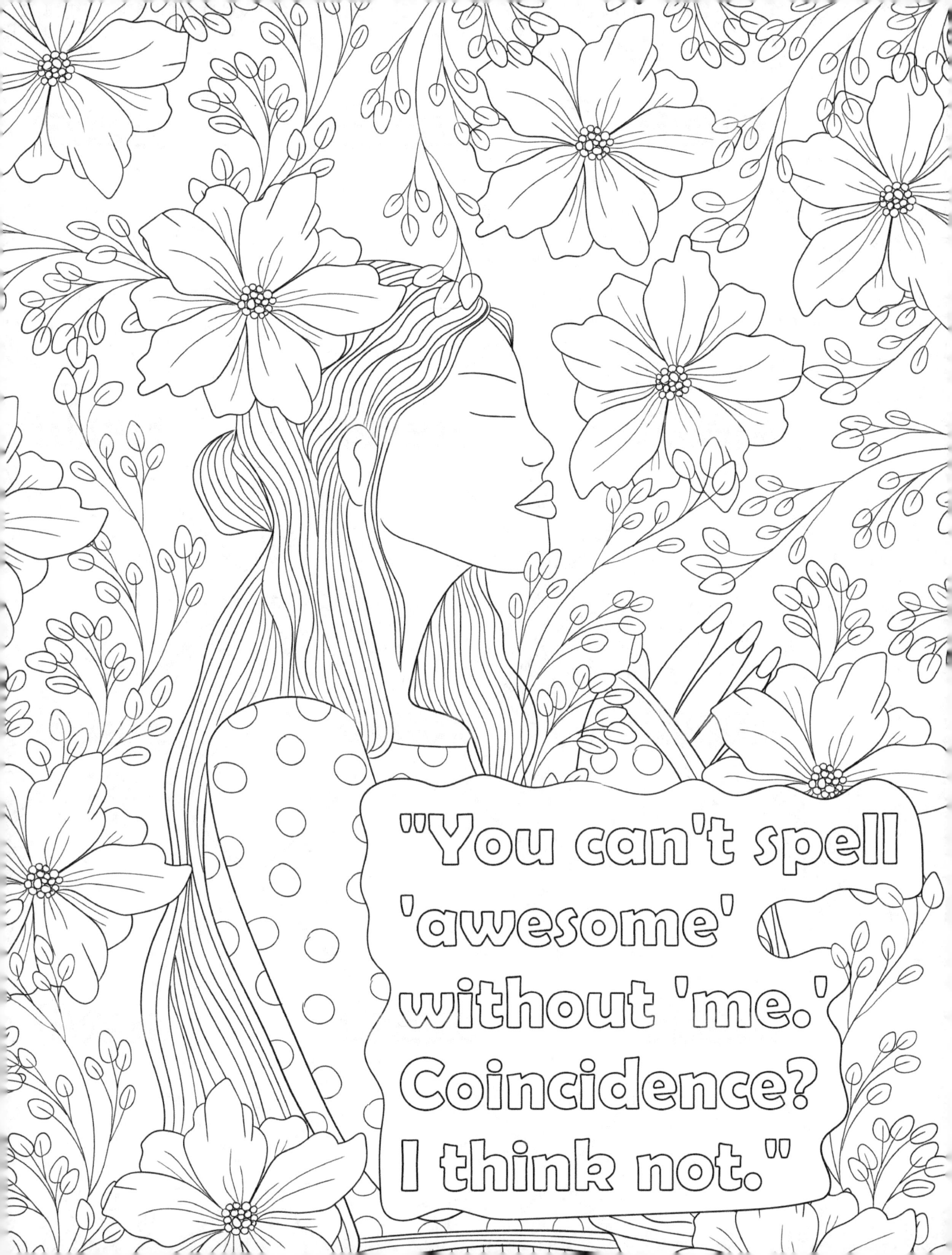

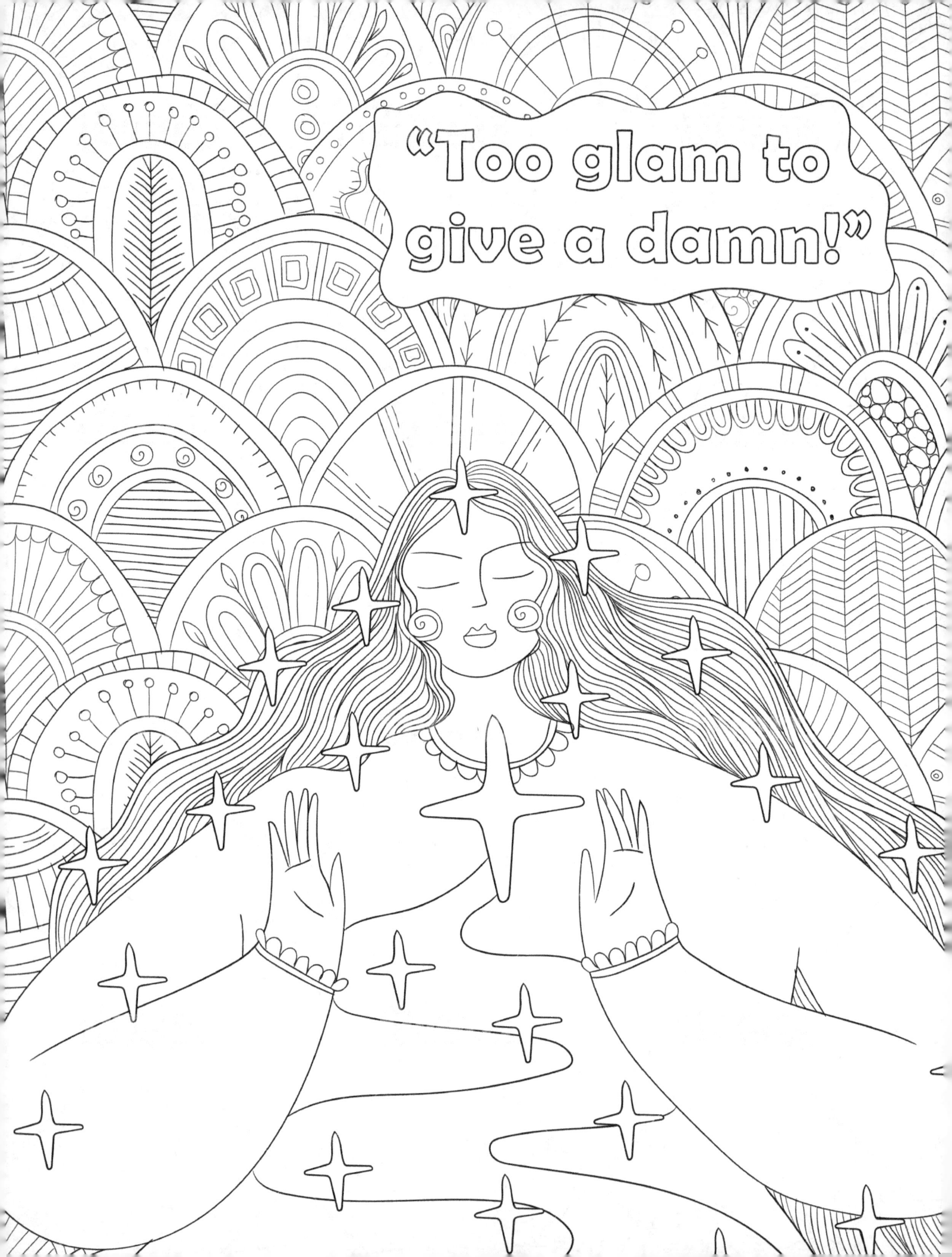

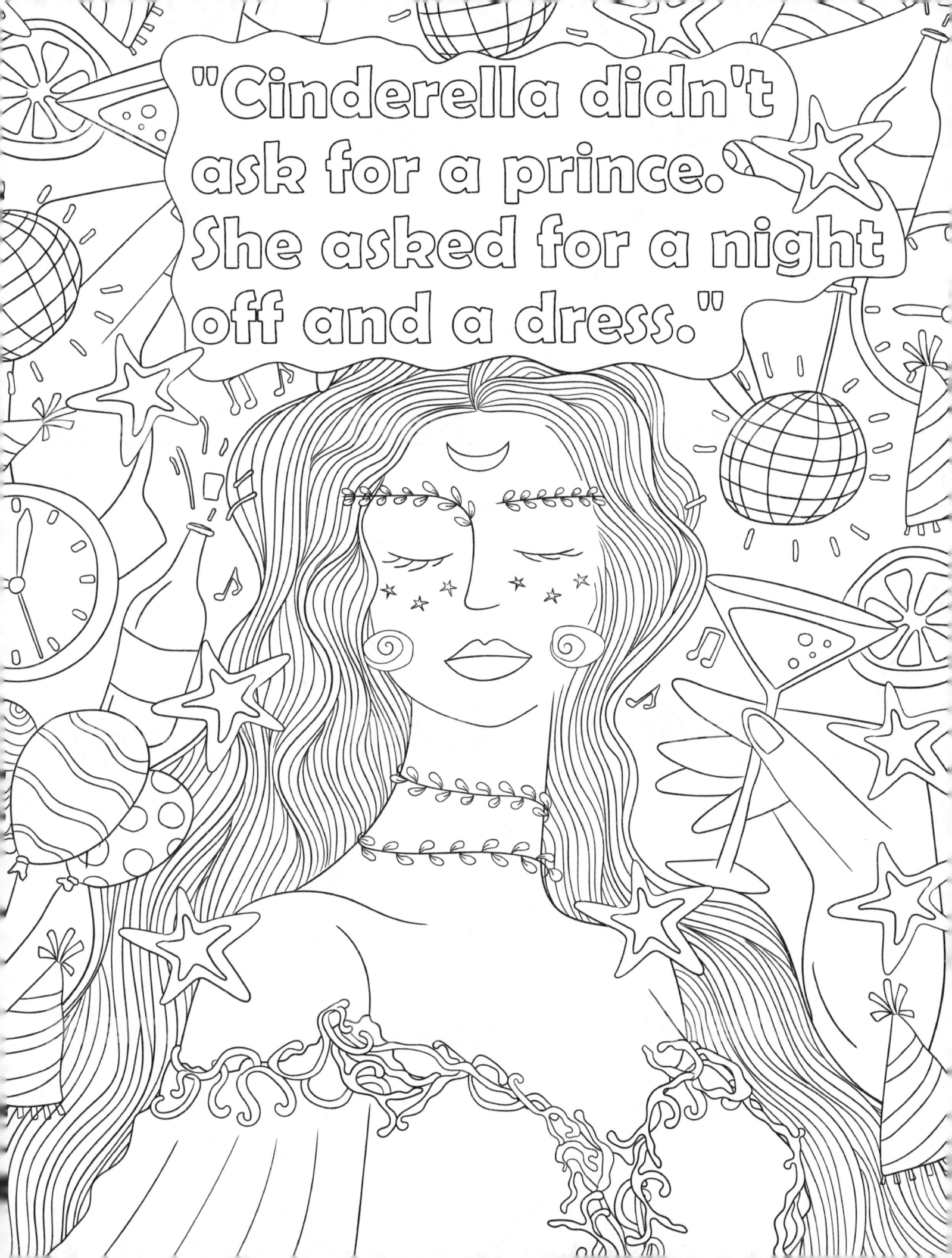

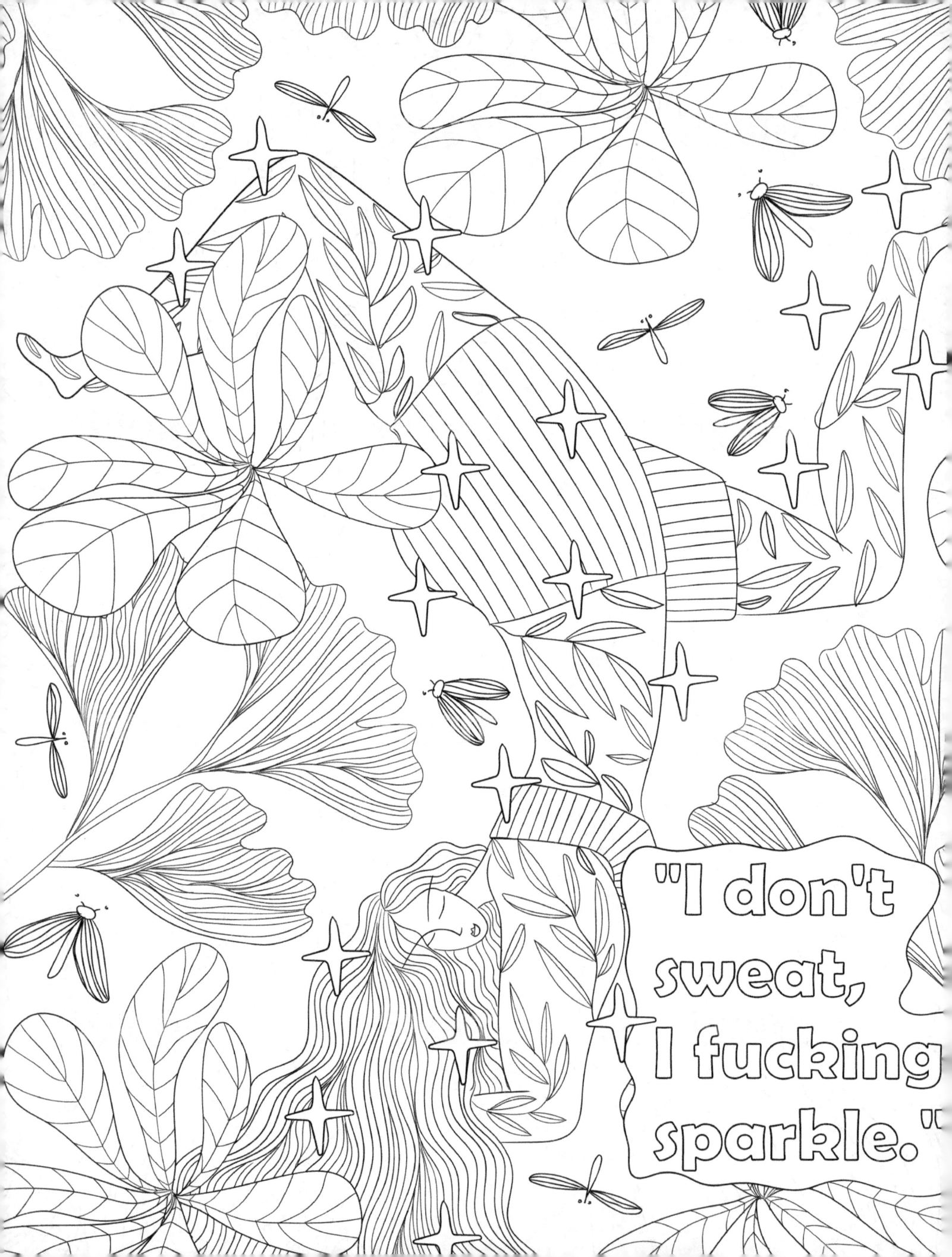

"I don't sweat, I fucking sparkle."

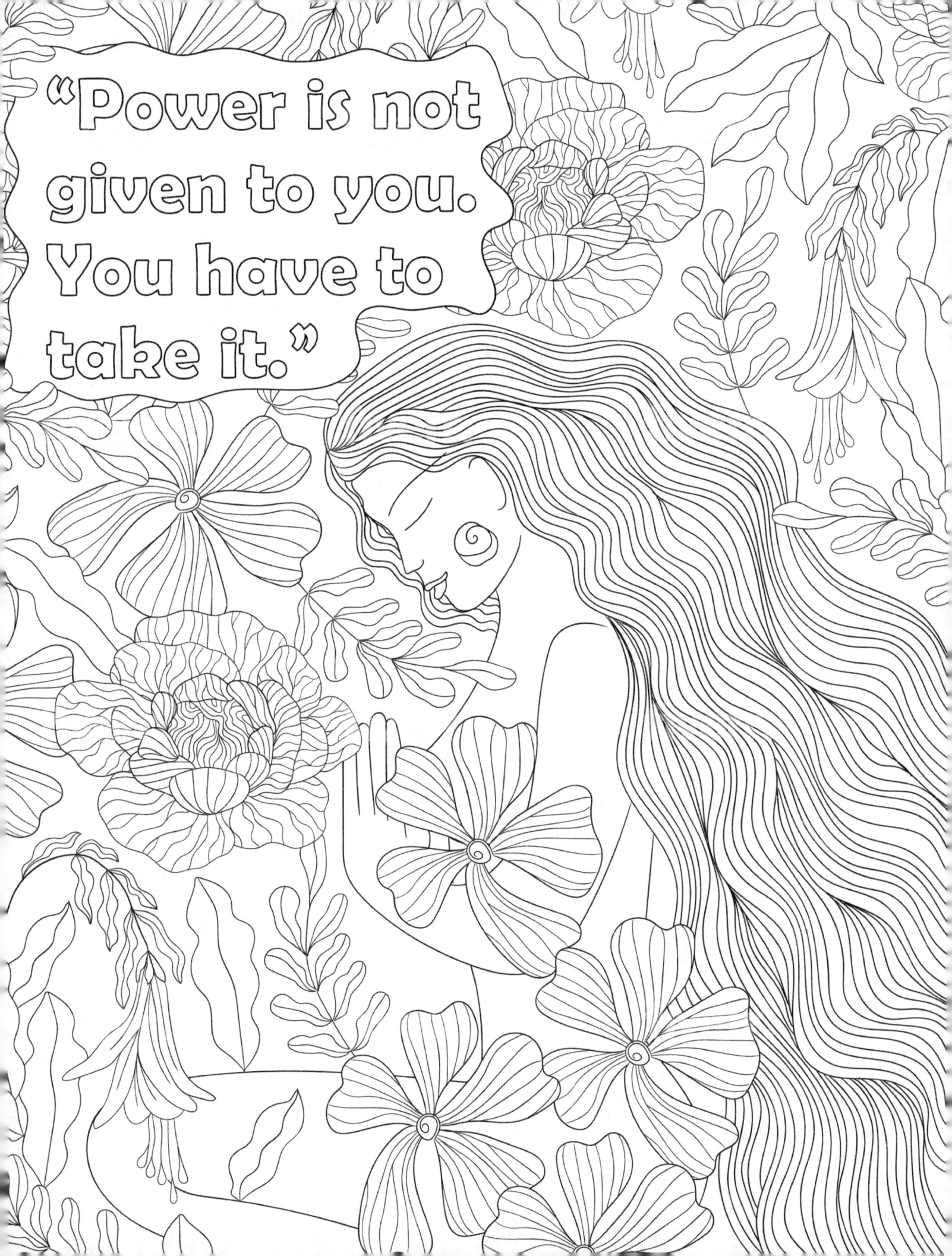

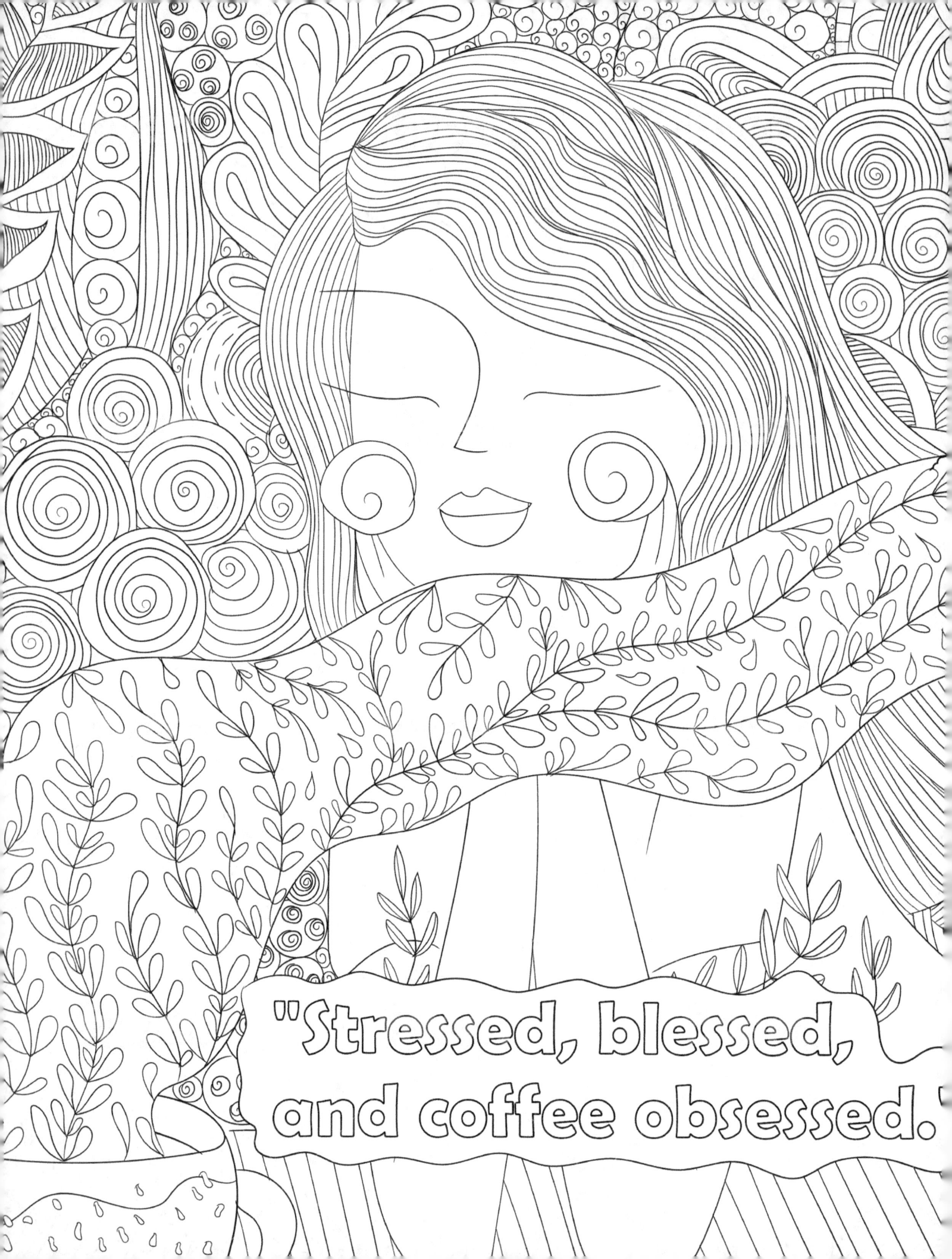

"Stressed, blessed, and coffee obsessed."

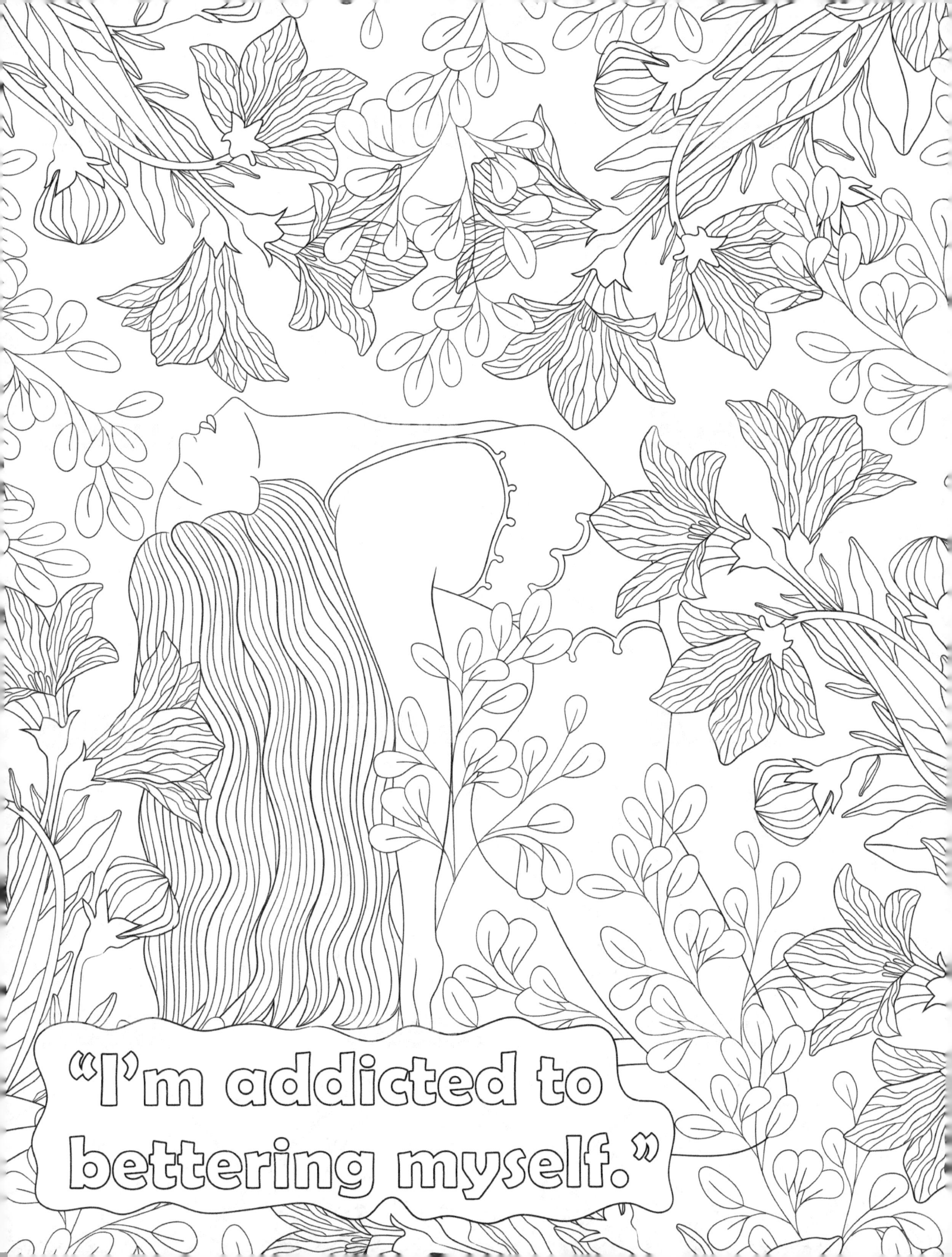

"I'm addicted to bettering myself."

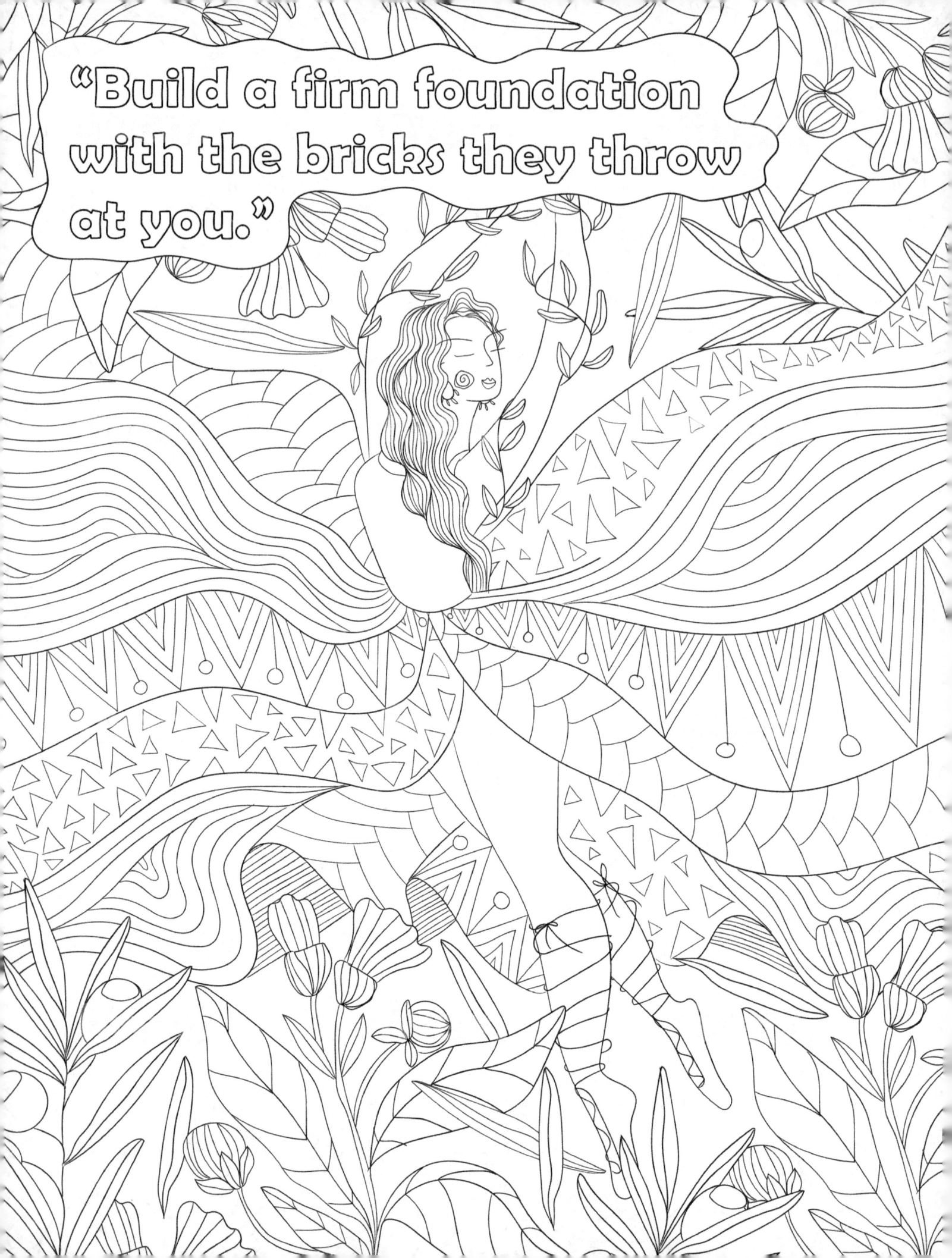

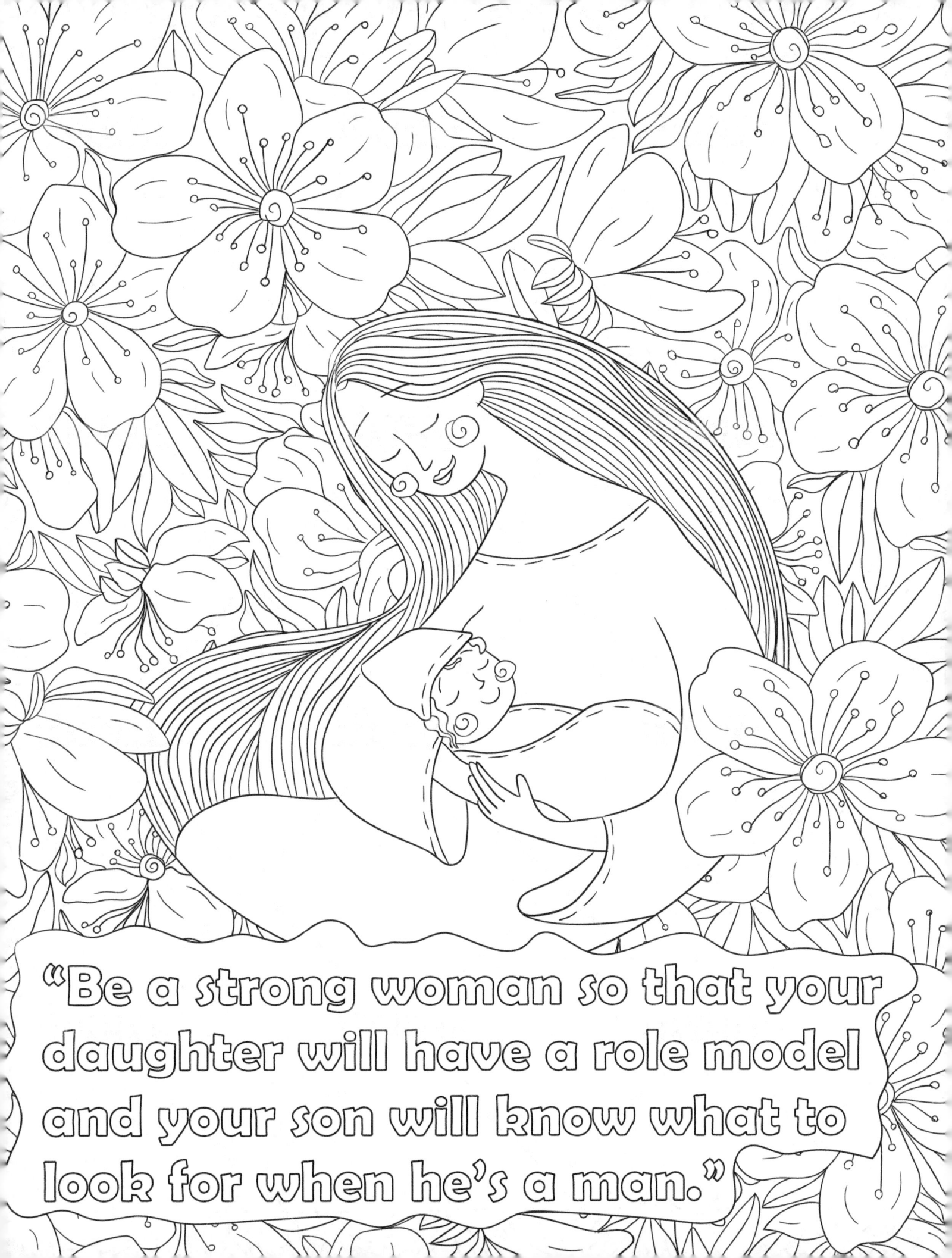

"Be a strong woman so that your daughter will have a role model and your son will know what to look for when he's a man."

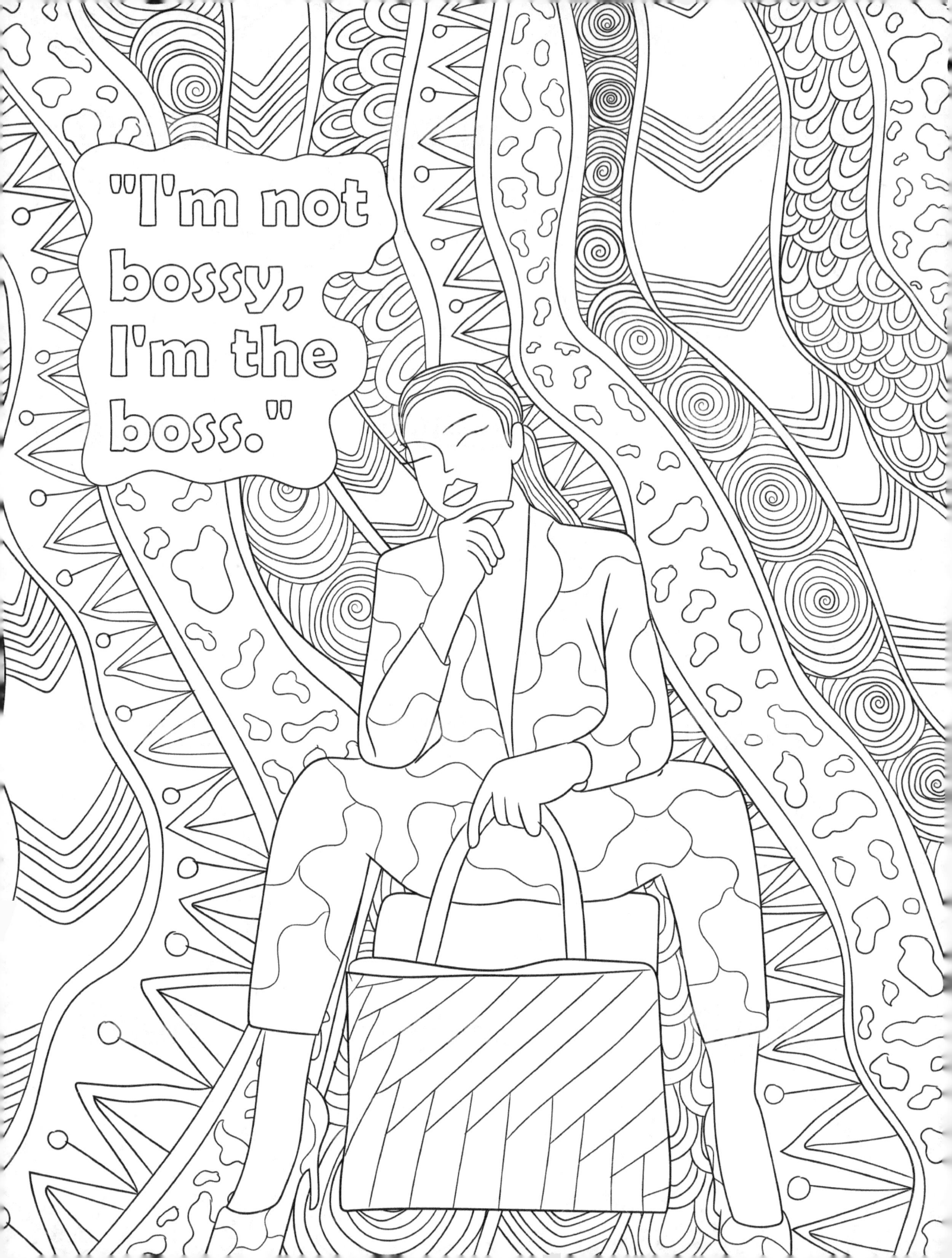

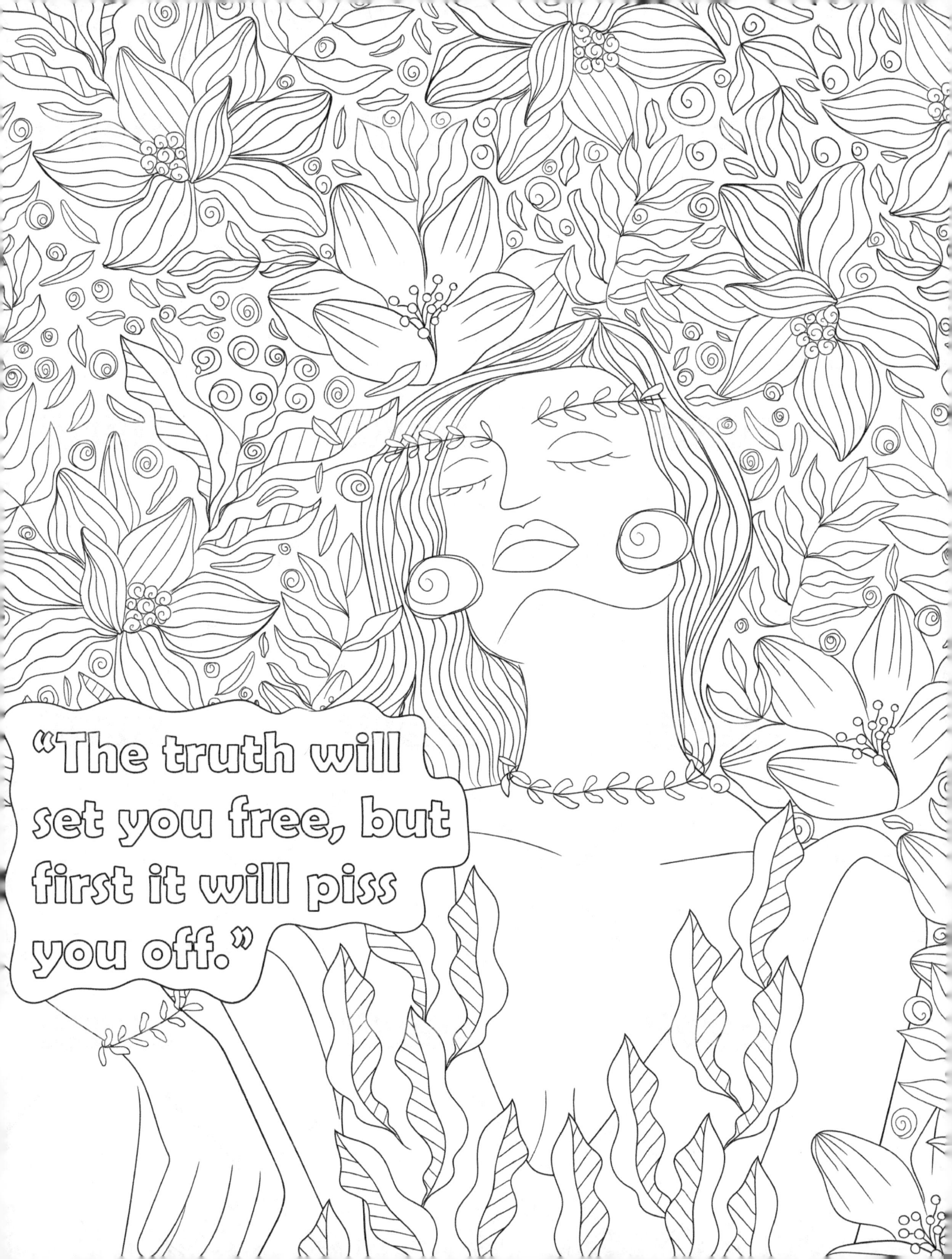

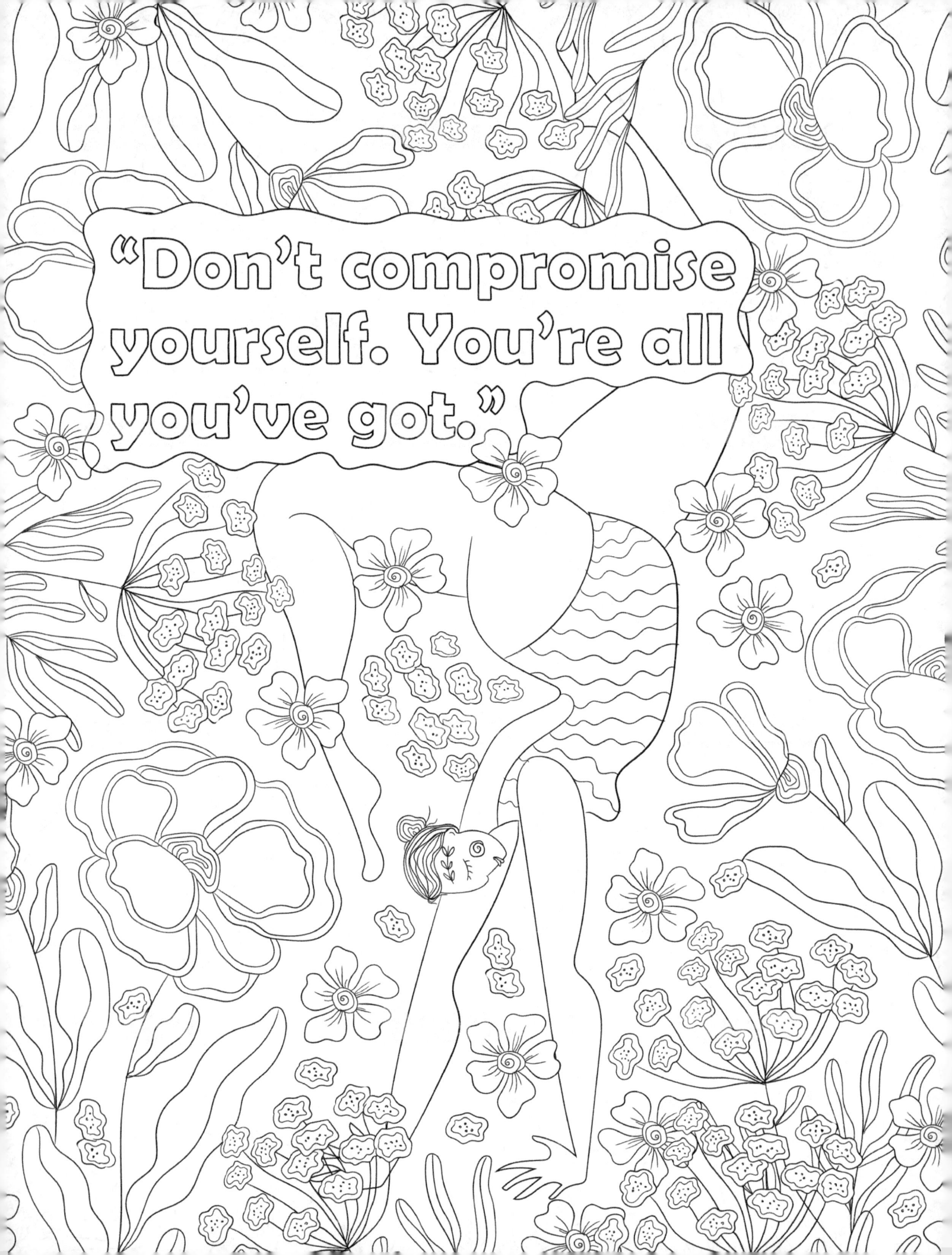

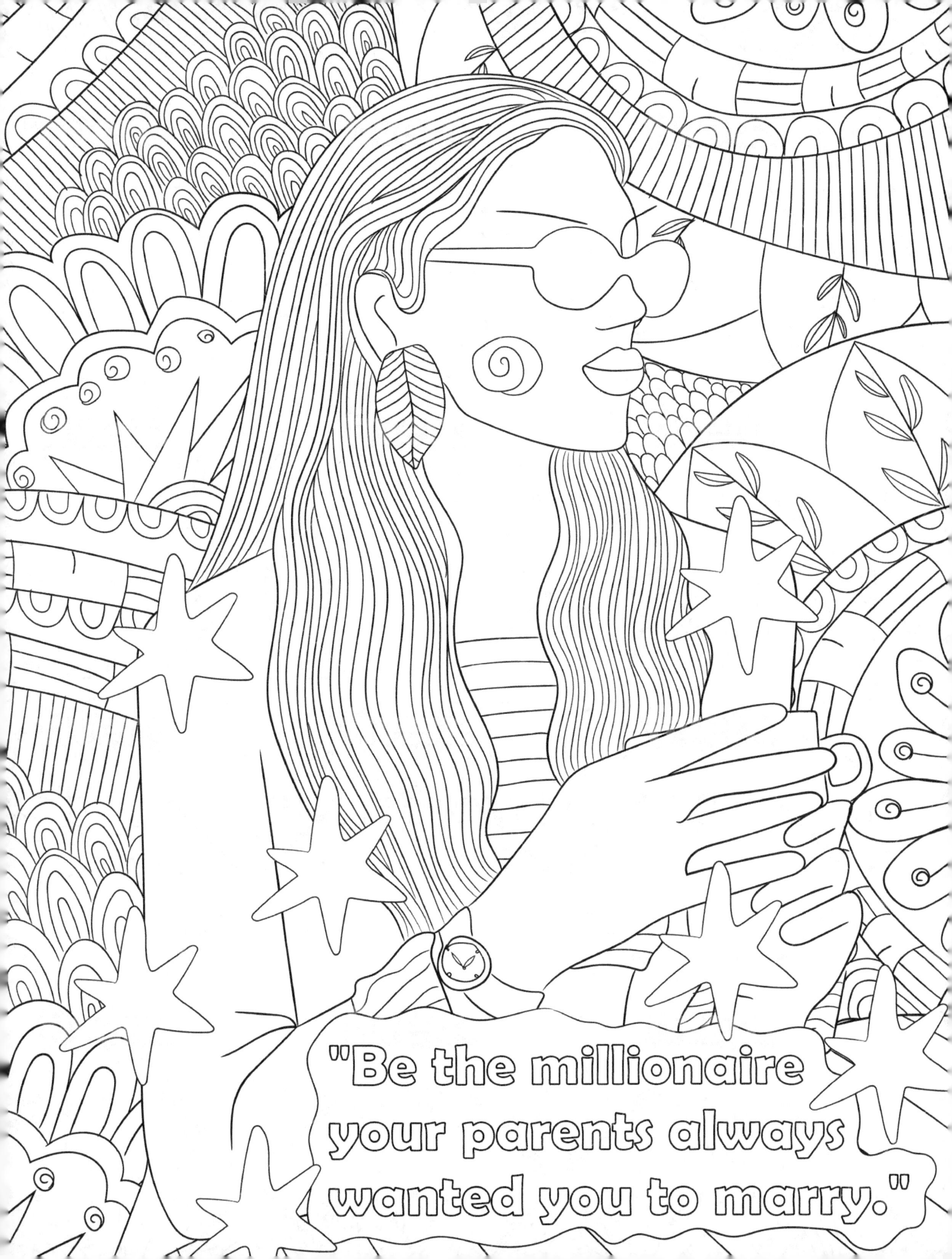

"Be the millionaire your parents always wanted you to marry."

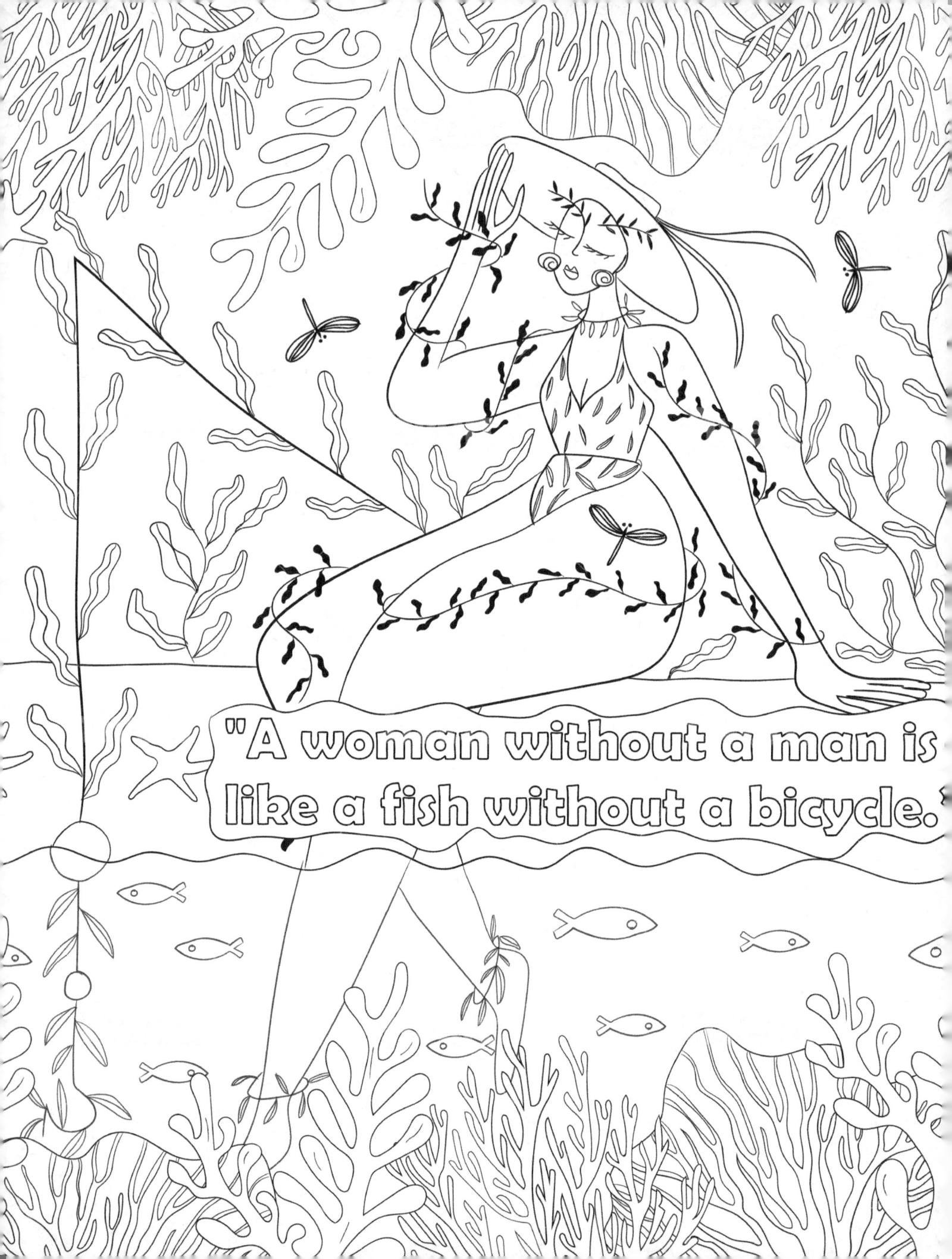

"A woman without a man is like a fish without a bicycle."

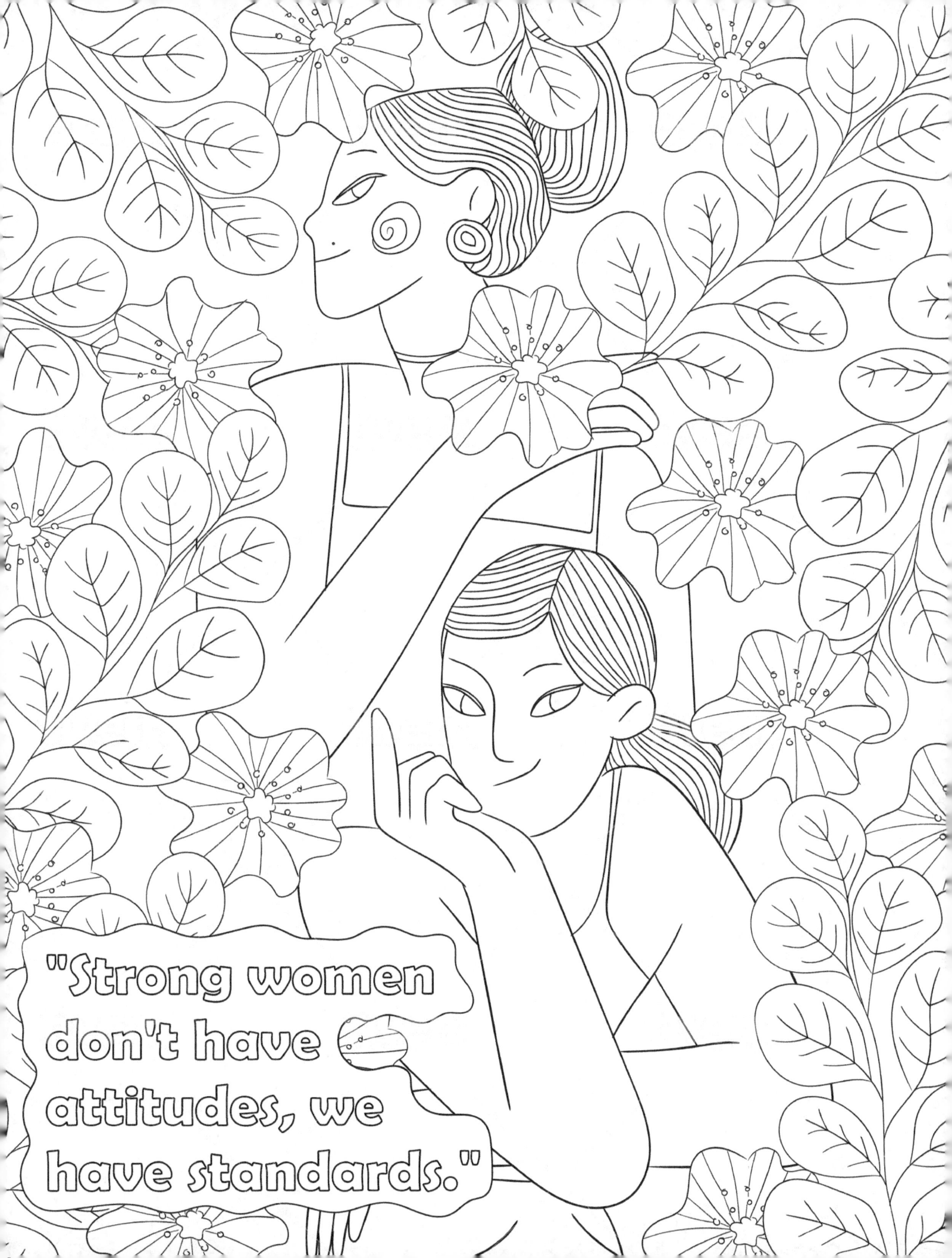

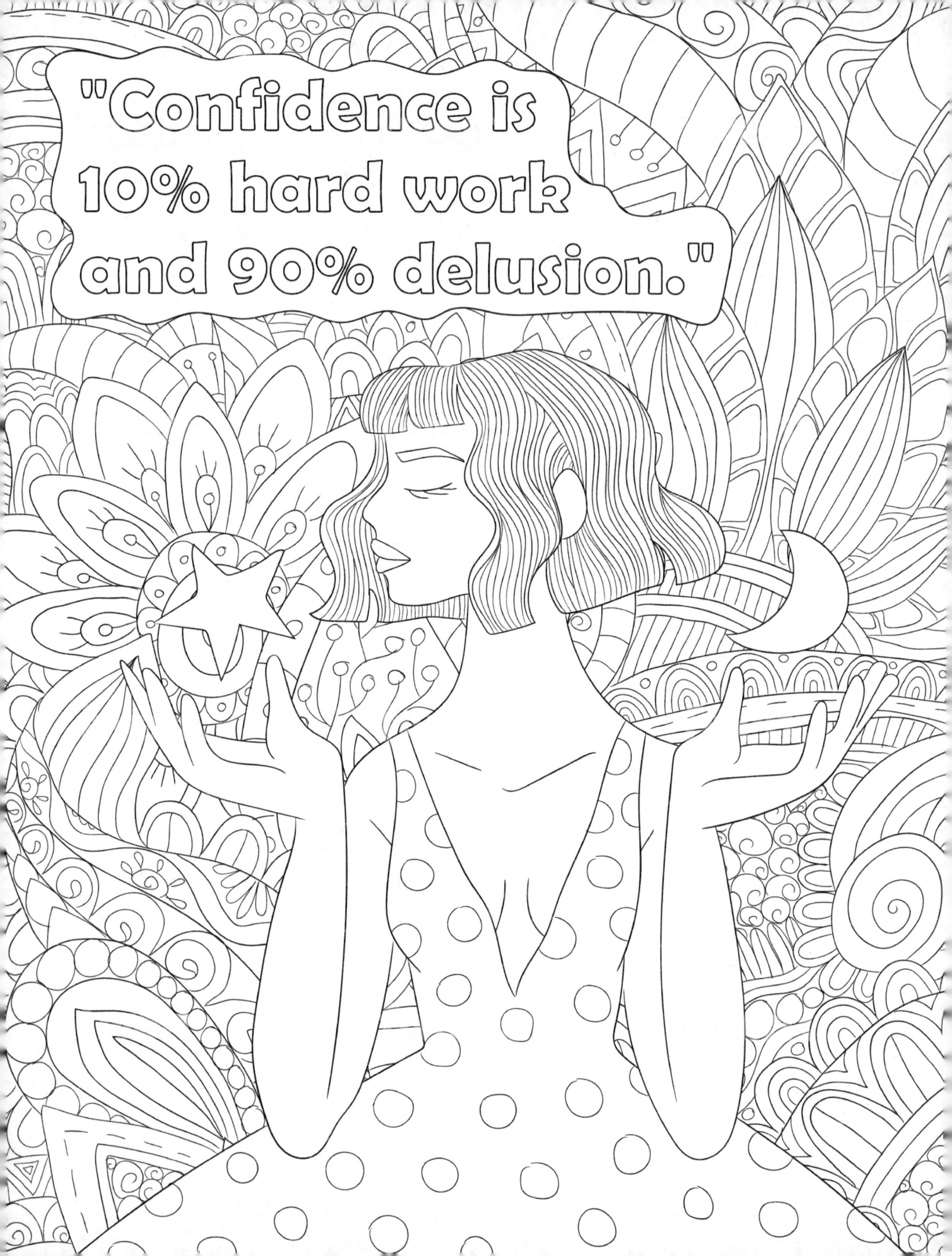

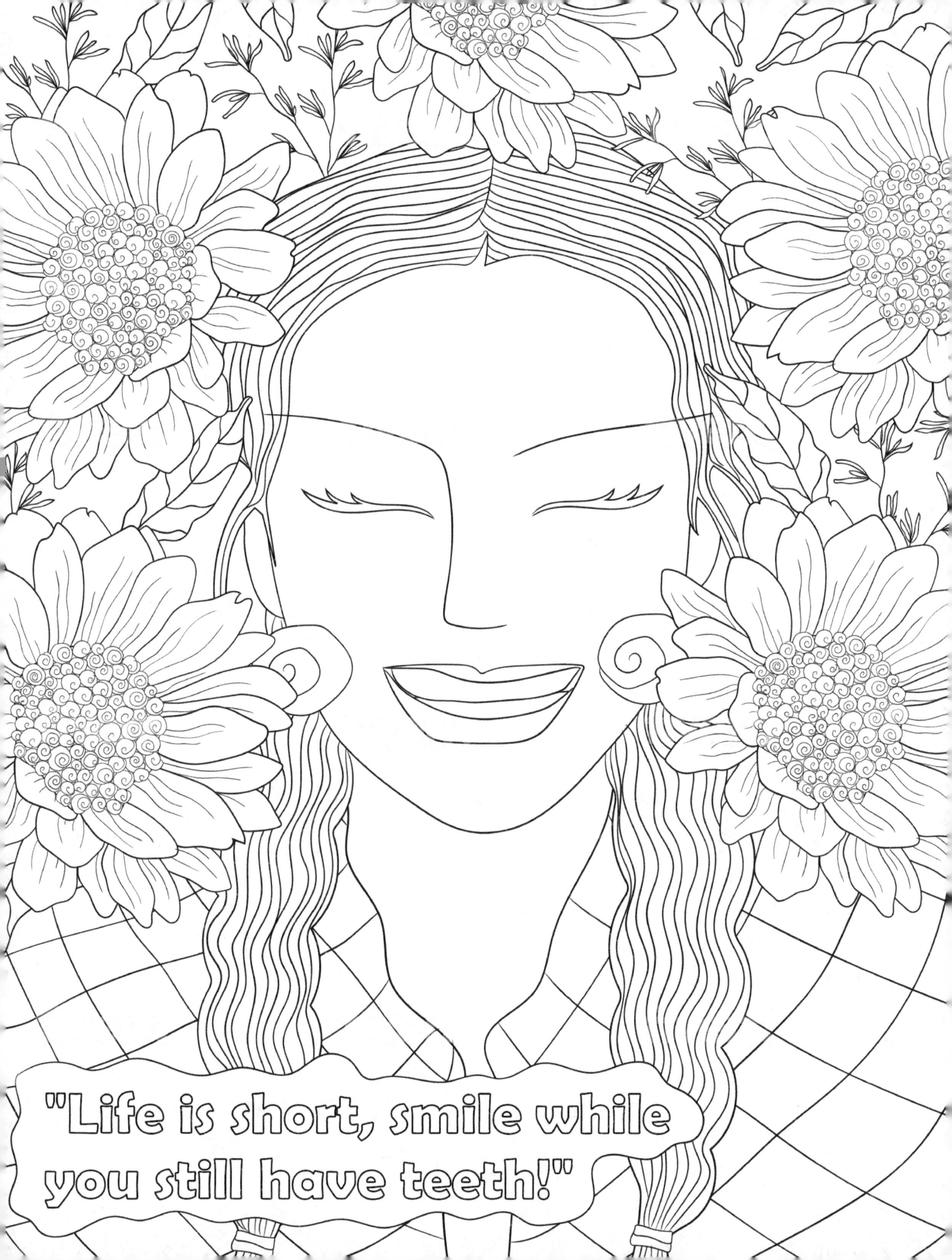

"Life is short, smile while you still have teeth!"

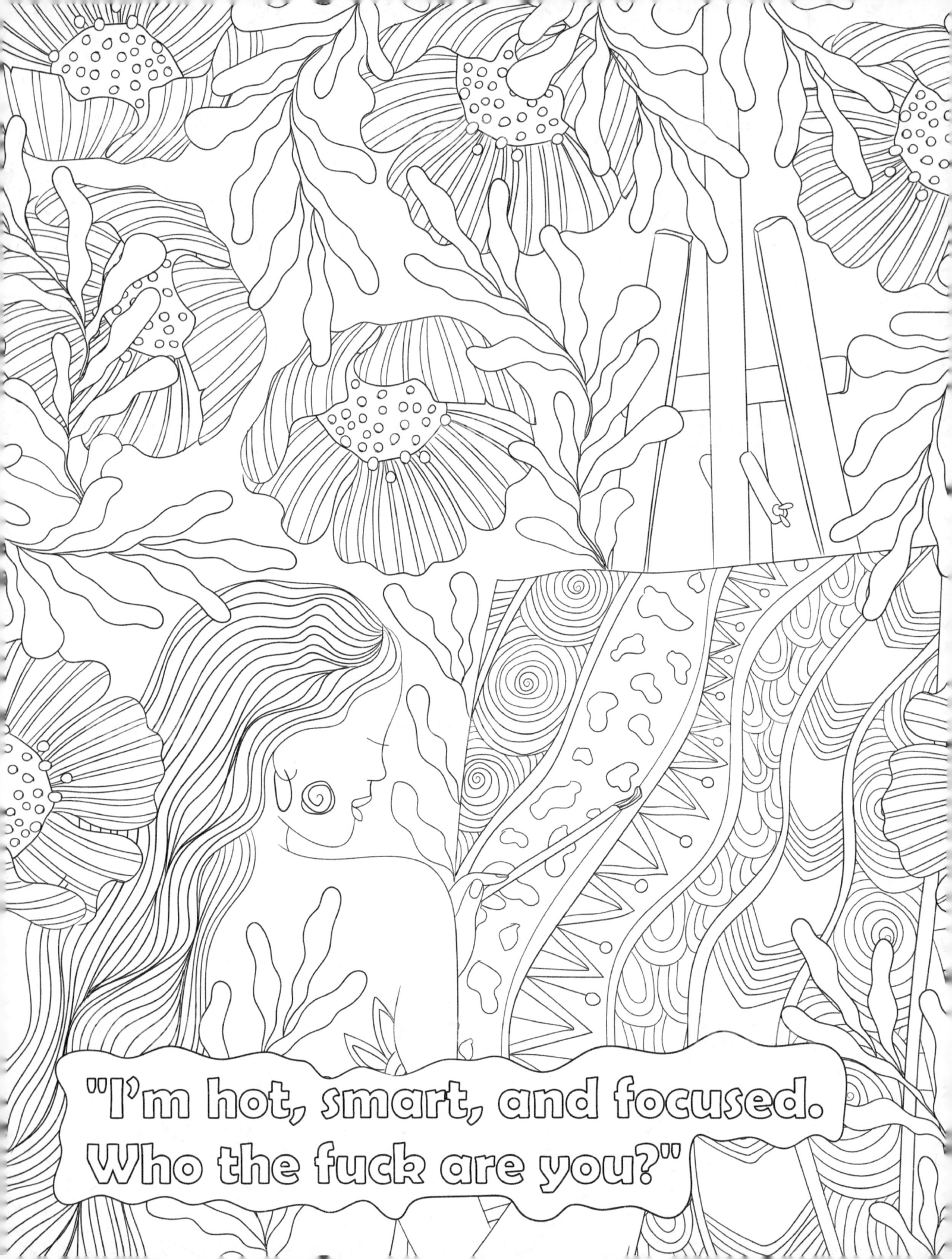

"I'm hot, smart, and focused. Who the fuck are you?"

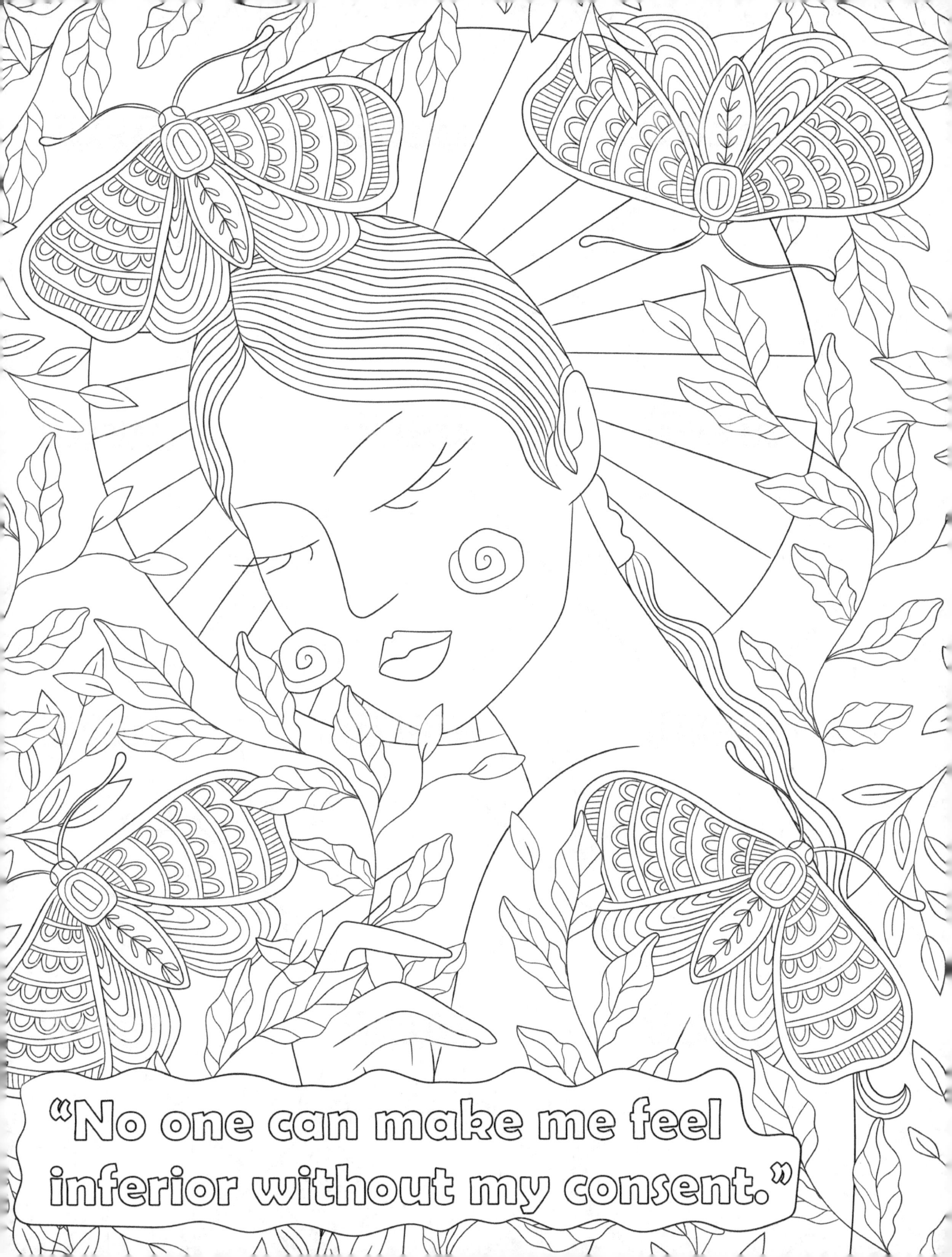

"No one can make me feel inferior without my consent."

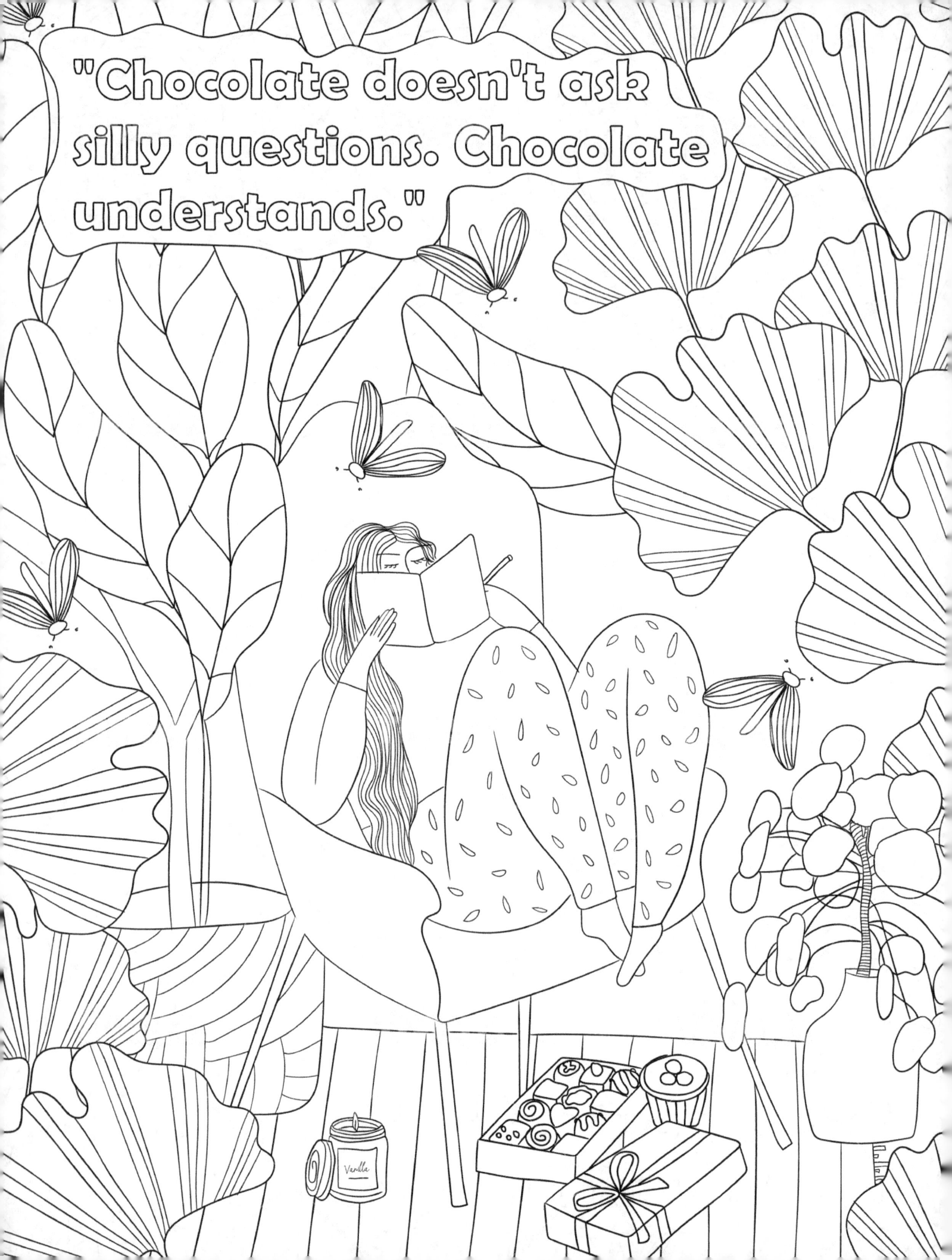

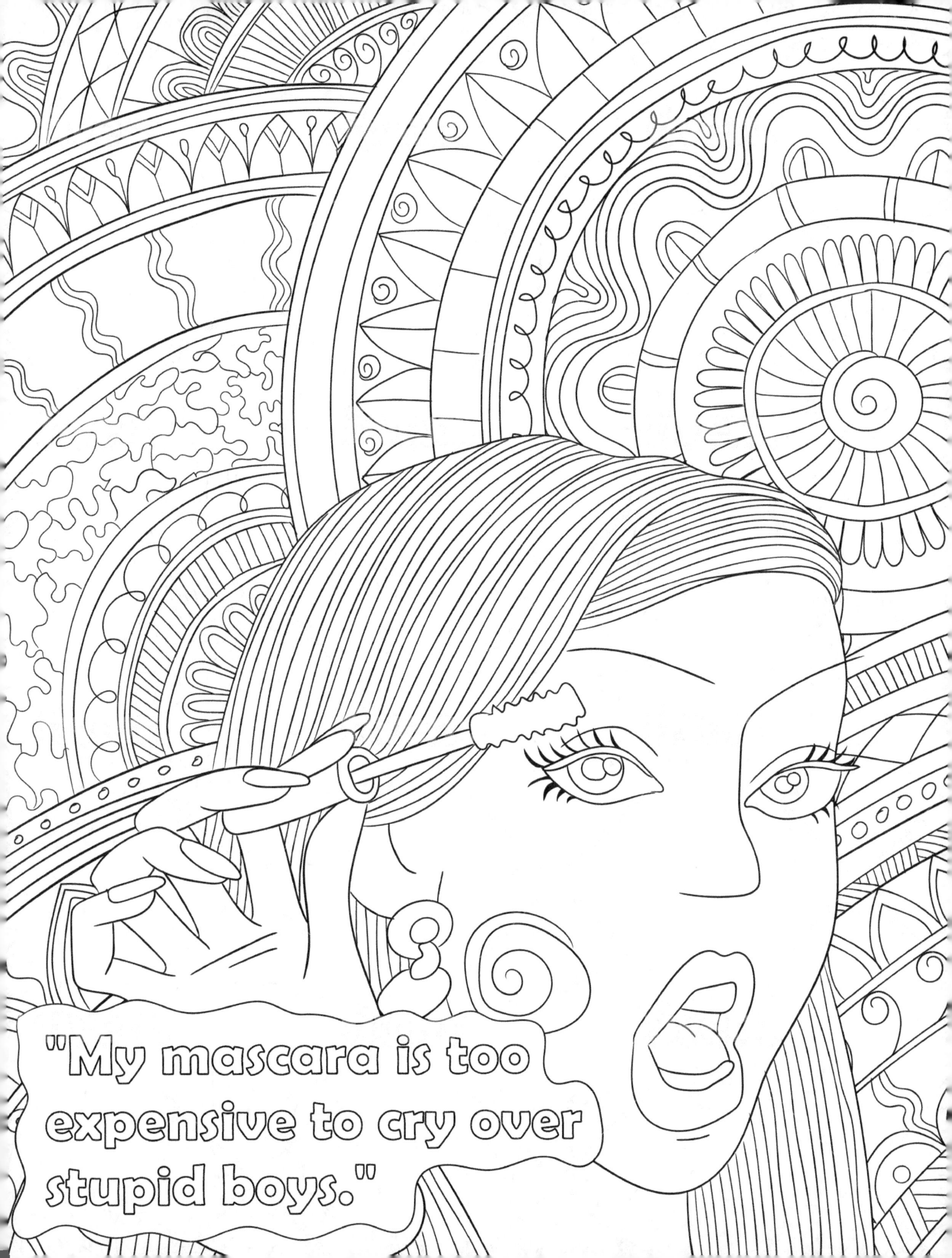

"My mascara is too expensive to cry over stupid boys."

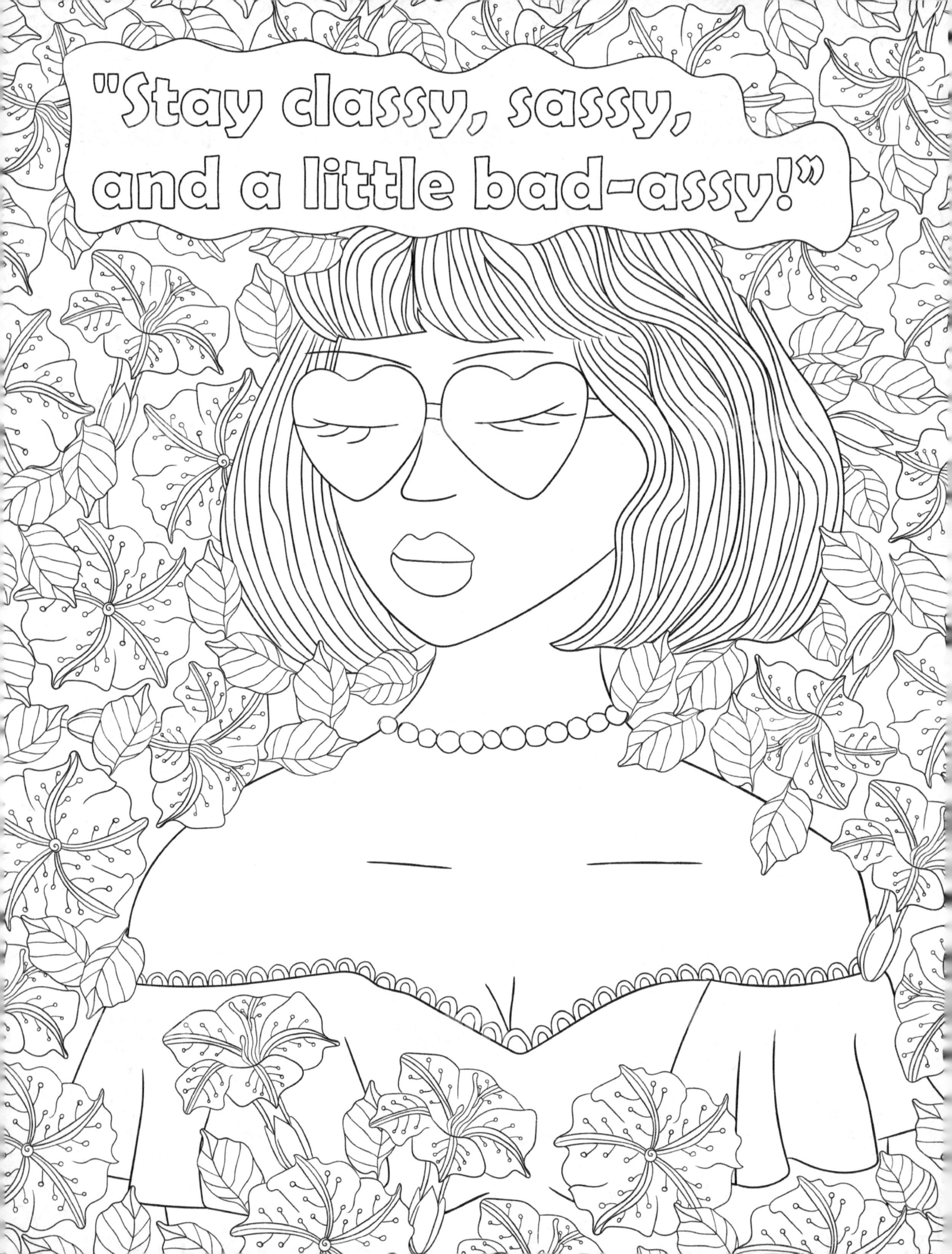

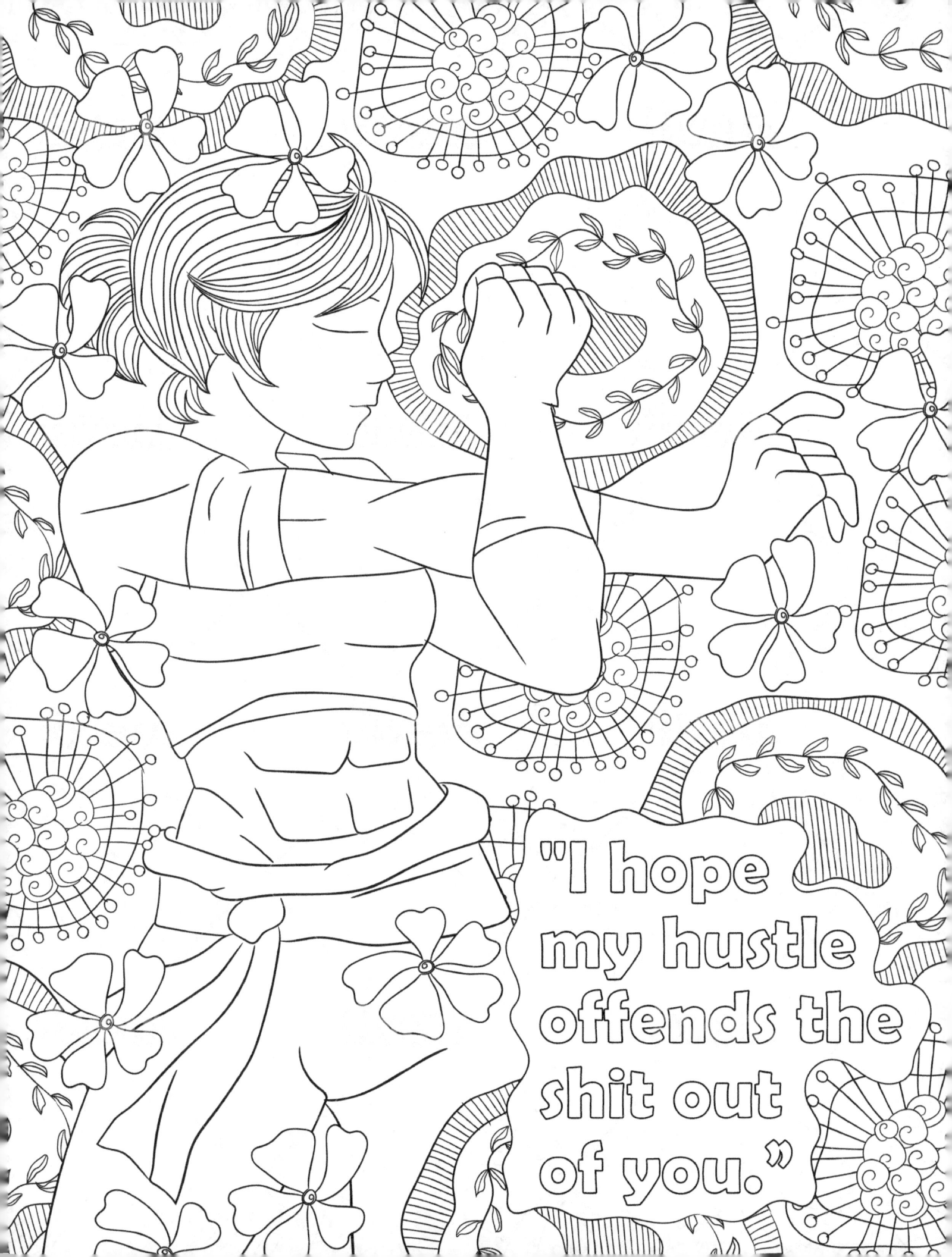

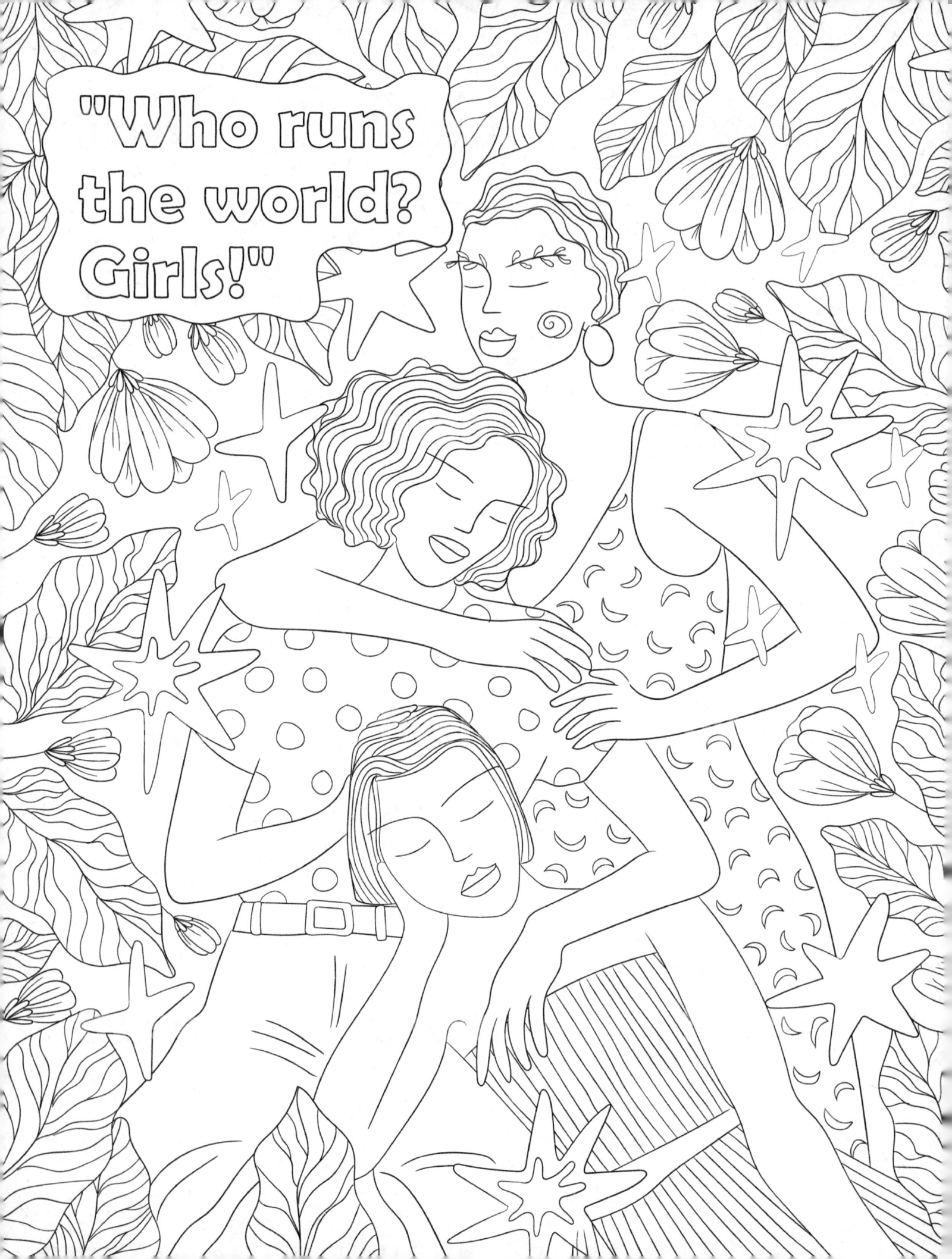

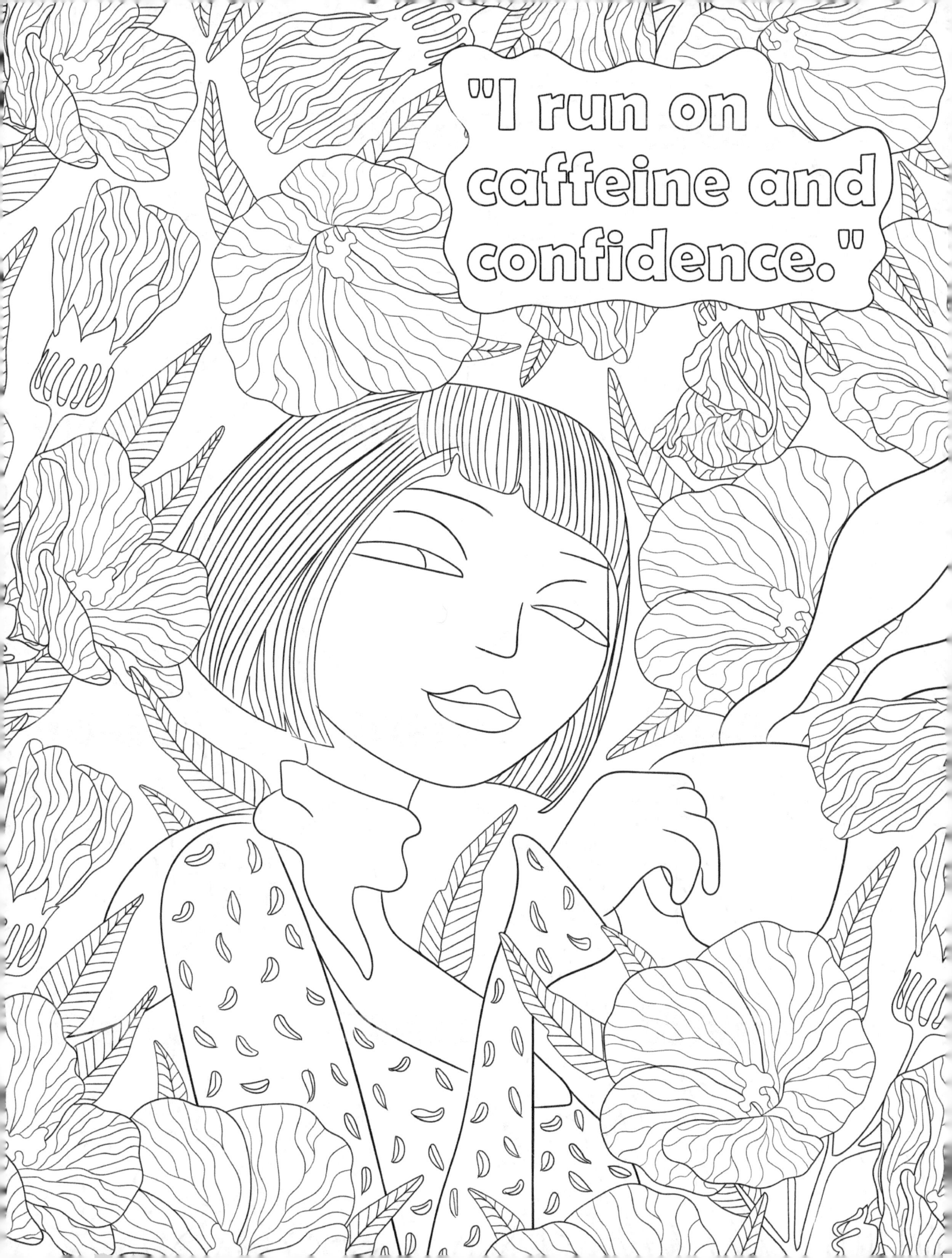

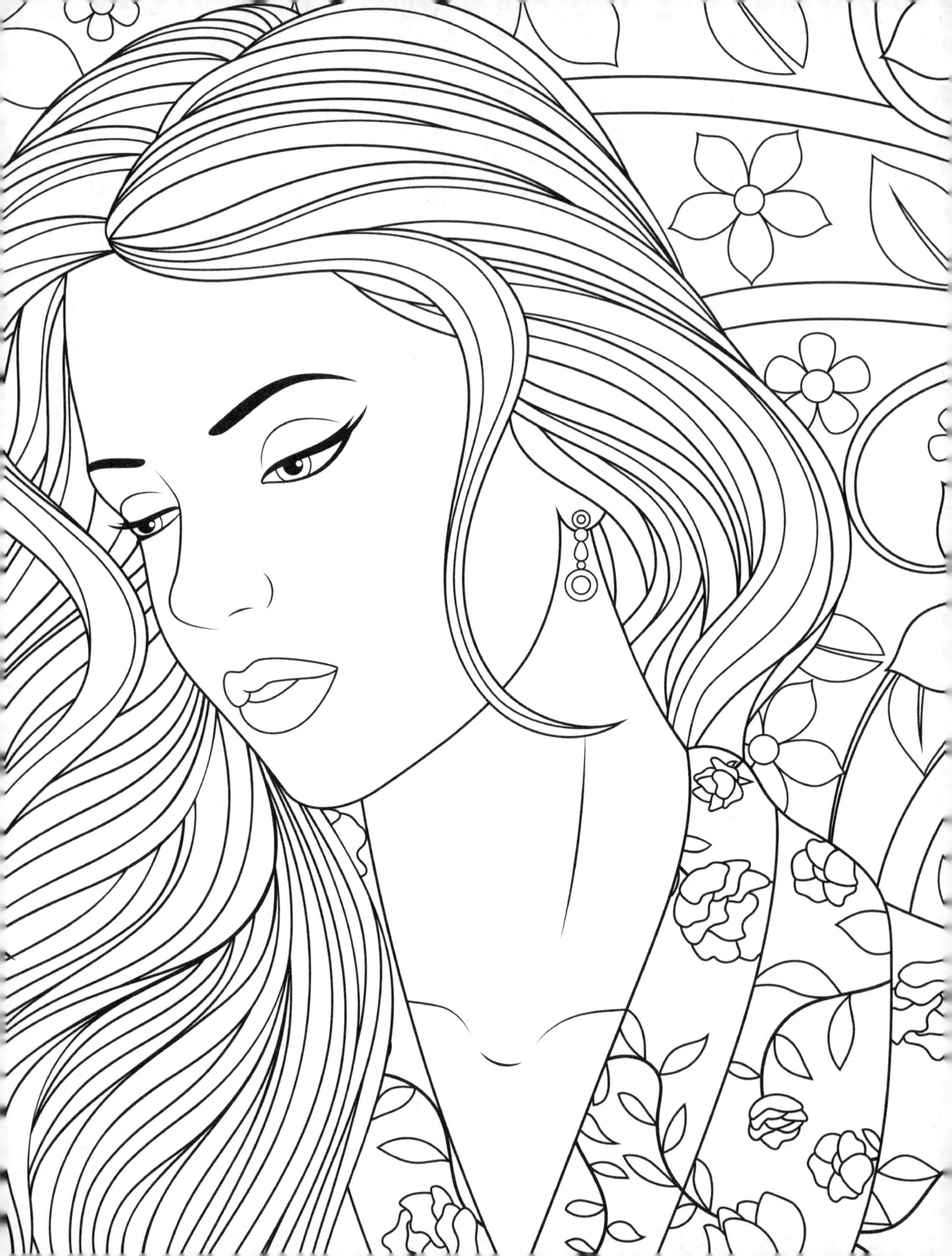

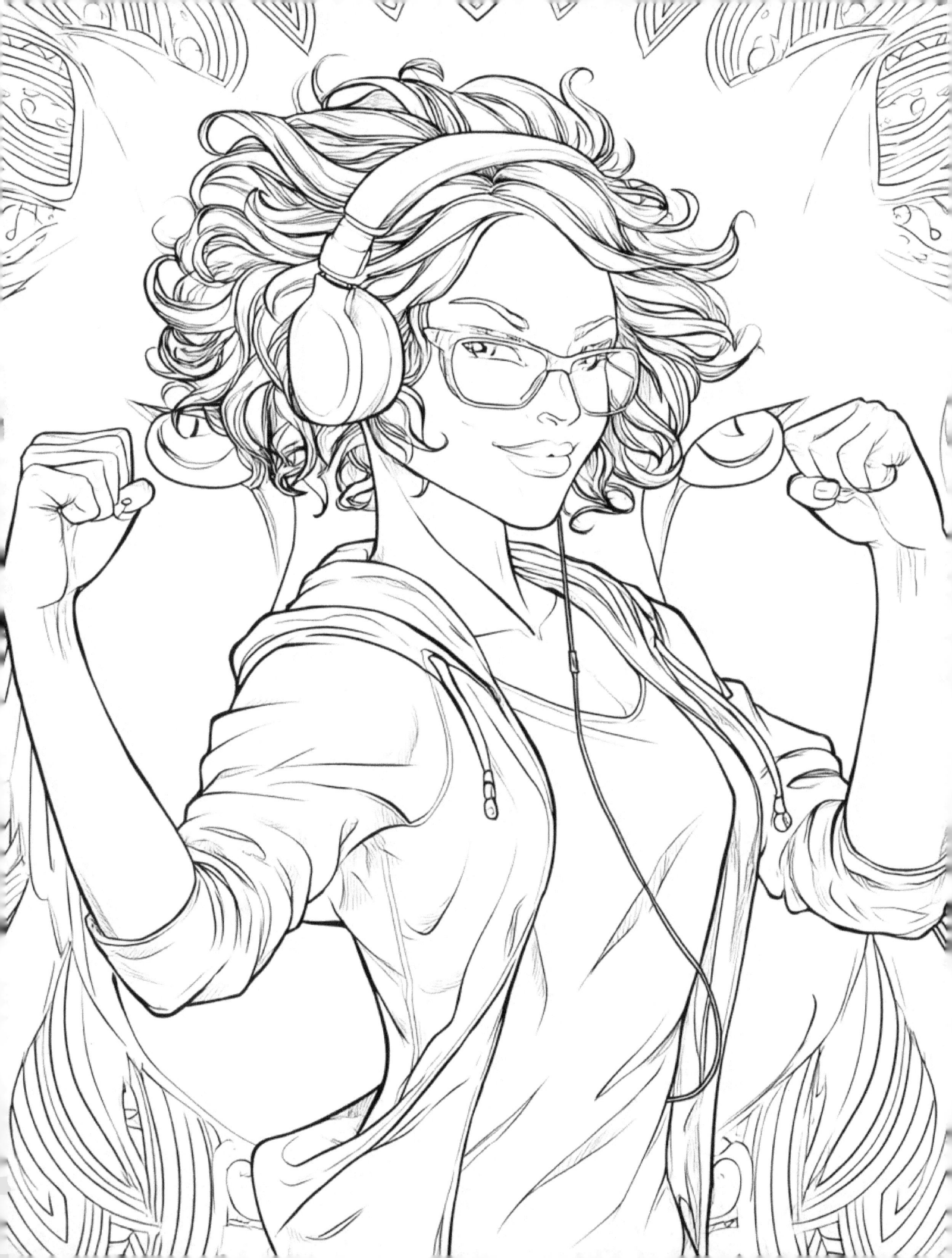

www.ingramcontent.com/pod-product-compliance
Lightning Source LLC
Chambersburg PA
CBHW081207170626
46811CB00011B/3341